No going back . . .

"Field hockey tryouts are on the south field. And—" Aaron stopped, inhaling deeply. "And if you stick around here at soccer tryouts, we're through," he finished flatly.

I felt as though I'd been slapped. All the air left my body.

"What are you talking about?" I almost whispered.

Aaron's stony expression didn't change. "Need me to repeat it? Fine. If you try out for the soccer team, our relationship is over."

I swallowed, fighting back all the pain that his words sent through me. If he could even give me such a ridiculous ultimatum, then I couldn't let him see how much losing him hurt me.

"Fine," I said coldly. "Don't bother to talk to me again. Ever."

Playing for Keeps

NINA ALEXANDER

BANTAM BOOKS
NEW YORK • TORONTO • LONDON • SYDNEY • AUCKLAND

RL 6, age 12 and up

PLAYING FOR KEEPS
A Bantam Book / October 1999

Cover photography by Michael Segal.

Produced by 17th Street Productions,
a division of Daniel Weiss Associates, Inc.
33 West 17th Street, New York, NY 10011.

ISBN: 0-553-49292-6

Published simultaneously in the United States and Canada

Bantam Books are published by Bantam Books, a division of Random House, Inc. Its trademark, consisting of the words "Bantam Books" and the portrayal of a rooster, is Registered in U.S. Patent and Trademark Office and in other countries. Marca Registrada. Bantam Books, 1540 Broadway, New York, New York 10036.

PRINTED IN THE UNITED STATES OF AMERICA

OPM 0 9 8 7 6 5 4 3 2 1

One

Claudia

"WHERE DID THE summer go?" I moaned, leaning my elbows on the table and running both hands through my hair.

Dad lowered the sports section of the *Washington Post* and grinned at me. "The game's not over till the buzzer sounds, Claud. You've got a good fifteen minutes of your summer vacation left."

I rolled my eyes. "Yeah, and the glass is half full, and every cloud has a silver lining, right?"

Dad shrugged his square, stocky shoulders and smiled. "I call 'em like I see 'em," he said with a wink.

I glanced at the clock that hung over the arched doorway of our kitchen. Mom had left for her law office half an hour earlier, and Aaron, my boyfriend, would be arriving any minute to pick me up.

"Anyway, maybe the buzzer hasn't sounded yet," I muttered, "but the game is already lost." I looked at the glass of orange juice I'd been nursing for the past twenty minutes and pushed it away with such force that it teetered and nearly spilled all over the rest of the newspaper, which was scattered across the middle of the table.

"Whoa, watch it, champ," Dad said, pushing most of the newspaper pages into a messy pile and then reaching for the coffeepot to pour himself a third cup.

"Sorry. I guess I'm a little nervous about soccer tryouts today."

"You?" Dad raised one eyebrow, which gave his face a comical look, like a bulldog with an attitude. "Nerves-of-steel Claudia Willoughby?"

"It's stupid, I know," I admitted. "But I had this nightmare last night that I kept messing up all my shots and somehow didn't get a starting position. I *have* to do well this season. The college scouts start looking at you when you're a junior. And I—"

I stopped short when I heard a horrible screeching sound from the direction of the street. It was followed by a couple of ominous thuds and then a loud, long hiss. The clanking, sputtering sound of Aaron's ancient green Ford pickup—a gift from his parents for his sixteenth birthday—was unmistakable.

"Sounds like Aaron's here." I stood and leaned over to give my father a quick peck on the cheek. "Wish me luck."

"You don't need it." Dad punched me lightly on the shoulder. "Tell Aaron I said hi."

I hurried out of the kitchen and down the front hall, pausing just long enough to check my reflection in the large oak-framed mirror near the door. I wasn't usually very concerned with clothes, but I'd chosen my outfit carefully that morning, and I was satisfied with the results. My favorite jeans were faded to perfection and fit snugly, and my white cropped T-shirt set off my dark eyes and lightly tanned complexion perfectly. I'd even forgone my usual ponytail, instead wearing my shoulder-length brown hair down in soft waves around my face.

I heard a honk from outside and quickly turned away, grabbing the duffel bag that held my cleats and a change of clothes for tryouts that afternoon. Taking a deep breath, I swung open the door, blinking a few times to adjust my eyes to the brilliant, warm sunlight of the gorgeous September morning. Aaron stood at the curb by his truck, scowling at some ugly black smoke that was spiraling out slowly from beneath the hood. I hurried toward him, pausing just long enough to wing the soccer ball lying on the walk in the direction of the garage. It bounced squarely off the middle of the door with a satisfying thump.

Aaron heard the sound and turned, his scowl changing immediately to a smile. "Looking good, Claud," he said, giving me an appreciative once-over before pulling me toward him for a good-morning kiss.

I kissed him back, feeling a familiar tingle from being close to him. "Mmm, good to see you too," I murmured against his lips.

After a moment he pulled away and brushed a stray strand of hair off my forehead. "Ready to head back to the old Randallstown prison for another year?"

"Ready as I'll ever be," I replied. As I stepped back I marveled at how even after nine months Aaron could still make my heart do this weird little flipping thing. A summer spent playing one-on-one soccer in my backyard, swimming at the town pool, and hiking in the state park had kept him in great shape. Plus all that time in the sun had given his short dark hair auburn highlights that framed his adorable face. Yanking my mind out of a fantasy of spending the entire day running my fingers through that hair, I glanced at the truck. Aaron had cut the motor, but the truck didn't seem to realize it—it was still letting off a soft *chunk-chunk-chunk* sound. "Is the mean green machine ready to get us there?"

"She'll pull it off somehow. Always does." He patted the pickup fondly on its battered hood, then hurried around to the passenger side to open my door for me. "Your chariot awaits," he announced in his best snooty-butler voice.

"When did you turn into such a gentleman?" I joked.

"I've always been a gentleman. You just never noticed."

"Yeah, right." I tossed my duffel onto the

patched leather seat of the truck and climbed in after it, automatically avoiding the sticky spot at the edge of the seat where Aaron's meathead older brother, Bruce, had dripped barbecue sauce a couple of weeks earlier. Aaron walked back around to the driver's side, and after a little coaxing on the clutch, he managed to bring the old truck back to life. Soon we were clanking and gasping our way down Commonwealth Street, skirting the edge of the state park that started across the street from my house. Before long we'd turned onto State Street and were heading for the big brick high school in the center of town.

I leaned back against the headrest, barely seeing the familiar sights of good old Randallstown, Virginia, slide past the window as I thought about how much had changed since the year before. "It's hard to believe that we didn't know each other this time last year," I mused in a sudden burst of nostalgia. "You were just some new guy."

"A studlike, totally brilliant new guy," Aaron corrected quickly as he shifted into fourth gear with the usual grinding, squealing sound. "Even then you couldn't take your eyes off me. Admit it."

"Excuse me, Mr. Egomaniac. Did you and Bruce switch brains or something?"

Aaron laughed. "You're assuming he has one to exchange," he replied with a wicked grin.

Aaron's brother was an awesome force on the football field—even I had to admit that—but he wasn't much of a human being off it. He was basically a Neanderthal who thought every girl on the planet wanted him and every guy wanted to *be* him. He was loud, crude, and obnoxious, and worst of all, he had absolutely no sense of humor about himself.

"Speaking of God's gift to football, how's he getting to school today?" I asked, remembering that Bruce's Mustang was in the shop that week, as it was about fifty percent of the time.

"He convinced Lisa to come over and pick him up." Aaron shot me a bemused half smile. "You know Bruce," he said. "All he had to do was ask, and she was practically begging to play chauffeur."

I snorted. "You almost sound proud of him."

"Well, you have to at least give the guy points for his nerve, right?"

I laughed weakly. Sometimes I suspected Aaron actually admired the brute, and it made me uneasy. I told myself it was some kind of sibling thing that, as an only child, I couldn't understand. But sometimes I wasn't so sure.

"Wow, I'm really going to miss summer this year," I murmured, feeling uncharacteristically sentimental as I thought back over the past couple of months.

"Yeah, no more making out on your back porch swing," Aaron said with a playful smile, reaching over to pat my knee.

I put my hand over his, squeezing his fingers. "Come on, Aaron. We're going back to school, not entering a convent."

"I certainly hope not," Aaron replied lightly as

he hauled the wheel around to make the left turn onto Cardinal Street. The green machine didn't have anything even slightly resembling power steering. "I look terrible in black. Besides, I'd really miss that old porch swing."

"Maybe tonight I should go to the movies or something so you and the swing can have some quality time alone together," I joked. "What do you think? You and the swing, the perfect couple."

"I don't know," he quipped back. "I don't think I could ever be serious about someone so unsteady—you know, always going back and forth on things."

I giggled. Aaron and I really brought out the silly side in each other. Of course, in Aaron's case the silly side wasn't buried too deeply. Before we'd met at a sports banquet sophomore year, my main knowledge of him had been as a guy who cracked jokes so often in our science class that the teacher had threatened to laminate a note to the principal. That way she wouldn't have to write out a new one each time she sent him off to the office for disrupting class.

"From now on we'll probably have so much homework every night, you'll forget what I look like," I muttered.

He shook his head. "Sorry, wrong answer." He slipped into his dead-on impression of a smooth, silver-throated announcer's voice. "But we have some lovely parting gifts for you. A year's supply of Turtle Wax, some Rice-A-Roni . . ."

I leaned over and punched him on the shoulder.

Aaron loved to tease me about my habit of watching game shows. I knew the shows were kind of stupid, but they certainly weren't any worse than the cheesy old monster movies Aaron liked—as I reminded him every chance I got. "Very funny," I said. "The way you're acting, anybody'd think you weren't even sad that summer is over."

He shot me a quick glance before returning his eyes to the road. "Summer, fall, what's the difference?" he said softly. "All that's important is that we're together."

My heart melted. Aaron was flip and funny most of the time, but sometimes he could be so sweet and caring that it blew me away. Unhooking my seat belt, I scooted across the truck's seat and impulsively threw my arms around him, knocking my duffel bag to the floor in the process. Unfortunately Aaron was taking the turn into the school parking lot at the time, and my bag landed on his foot, causing it to slip off the gas pedal. The truck let out a loud backfire and then stalled, completely blocking the entrance as well as one lane of traffic on the street. Horns started blaring immediately, but I didn't care.

"You're the greatest, did you know that?" I told him, squeezing him as tightly as I could before pulling back just far enough to bend my head and kiss him.

He was smiling as his lips met mine. "I try," he murmured.

"Claudia! There you are!"

I turned from helping Aaron try to cram my

duffel into my new locker and saw Jenna Stevens running toward me. Jenna had been my best friend since second grade, when we'd both been forwards on the same community soccer team—Pete's Plumbing Panthers. I hadn't seen Jenna since the end of July, since her family spends every August at their beach house. But I could tell that this wasn't the time to ask about her vacation. Jenna looked and sounded even more breathless than usual—her round, apple-cheeked face was the same shade of crimson as the tank top she was wearing with her trademark baggy jeans, and her curly reddish brown hair was flying out from her head in all directions.

"What's wrong?" I asked when Jenna reached us. "You look like you've been running laps or something. Tryouts aren't till this afternoon, remember?"

Jenna panted out a quick hello to Aaron, then grabbed my arm. "Haven't you heard?" she exclaimed. "I can't believe it. I mean, I *believe* it, but only because I know for a fact that it's true—Coach Spooner told me herself. But I still can't believe it—it's just *too* awful. And how could they, after the incredible season we had last year. I mean, we even beat Westville, and we *never* beat Westville. And—"

"Focus!" I shouted, interrupting Jenna's stream-of-consciousness monologue. "What are you talking about?"

She blinked. "Oh. Sorry."

Aaron grinned. "Jenna, a word of advice. Never decide to become a TV newscaster, okay? The United States could declare war against Canada and nobody would ever know it if they had to rely on you to tell them."

Jenna rolled her eyes, and I chuckled. "So what's your big news?" I asked her.

"You don't even want to know."

"Okay, then," Aaron said teasingly, turning as if to head down the hall. "Time to get to homeroom."

I elbowed him in the ribs, quickly losing my tolerance for his goofy sense of humor. Jenna's expression was starting to worry me.

"Tell me," I demanded.

"It was because of budget cuts, I think." She took a deep breath. "They're cutting the soccer team." With a quick glance at Aaron, she quickly added, "The girls' team, I mean. Cutting as in canceling, deleting, exterminating. All gone." She drew one finger across her throat to illustrate.

I was stunned. I didn't know what I'd been expecting, but it wasn't this. "They can't do that!" I blurted out in disbelief.

"You're not serious." Aaron sounded just as shocked and horrified as I felt. "Why would they do something so stupid?"

"Don't ask me." Jenna shrugged. "Remember, this is the same school system that decided it was a good idea to paint the whole school puke green." She waved a hand to indicate the revolting color of the lockers and walls surrounding us. "Who knows how they think?"

"They can't," I insisted, my dreams of a soccer career vanishing right before my eyes. "It must be illegal to cut the girls' team and keep the guys' team, right? I'll get Mom to sue the school."

Jenna was chewing her thumbnail, a bad habit she'd never really been able to break. "I don't think so, Claud. As long as there are the same number of guys' and girls' teams, you've got no case. And guys don't play field hockey, remember?"

"Girls don't play football," I countered, unwilling to give up on my easy solution.

Aaron cleared his throat. "Cheerleading," he said in a hollow voice. My heart sank, realizing what he meant. "There are no guys on the squad—never have been," he continued. "So technically you would have to say it's a girls' sport."

I collapsed against the row of lockers behind me like a puppet whose strings had just been clipped. "But I saw Coach Spooner last week," I said blankly. "She didn't say anything about this."

"She didn't *know* anything," Jenna said. "They just told her yesterday."

As my initial shock and surprise wore off, a new feeling rose to take its place: anger. Pure, boiling, righteous fury. "They can't do this," I said fiercely. "We've got to do something."

"We could talk to the principal," Aaron suggested. "Start a petition or something. Maybe one of those radical types like Sam Wrightfield or Leo Lanier will put together a sit-in for us."

I suspected he was half kidding—about the sit-in part, at least—but it didn't seem like a joking matter to me. "We can't let it happen," I said.

Jenna sighed and shook her head. "It's already happened. We didn't even get a vote. There's no way they'll listen to us now."

I couldn't believe she was giving up that easily. Where was her fighting spirit, the fire that had always made her such a daring and determined soccer player?

"But what are we supposed to do if we can't play soccer?" I demanded.

What are we supposed to do if we can't play soccer? The words echoed in my head even as I said them, sounding foreign and strange and . . . impossible. What was I supposed to do if I couldn't play soccer? That was like asking what I was supposed to do if my heart couldn't beat.

Jenna shrugged and pushed a stray curl out of her eyes. "There's always field hockey," she said dejectedly.

"No way." I felt my fists clenching involuntarily at my sides. The anger was coursing through me more strongly than ever, white-hot and bubbling. It wasn't fair. "I don't play field hockey. I play *soccer.* How will any of the college scouts find me if I'm not even *playing* this year?"

Aaron put a hand on my arm. "I'm with you, Claud. This really stinks," he said tentatively. "But it doesn't sound like there's much we can—"

I shook off his hand with a jerking motion. "I want to play soccer," I said stubbornly. "I'm going to play soccer, no matter what those idiots on the school board say."

"Give it up, Claudia." Jenna was one of the only

people who could get away with talking to me in that tone. "It's hopeless. The Randallstown High girls' soccer team is dead."

"Fine." As she spoke, I realized what I had to do. It was so clear that I couldn't believe I hadn't thought of it right away. I folded my arms across my chest. "Then I'll just have to try out for the boys' team."

Two

Aaron

SHE MEANT IT. I knew right away that she meant it. She wore her crazed-kamikaze expression, which meant that her mind was made up and nothing short of a nuclear explosion was going to change it. Maybe not even that.

"Don't expect me to chip in for the sex-change operation," I said, trying desperately to turn the whole thing into a joke.

Claudia completely ignored my attempt at humor, which was probably just as well for me. "It's the only answer," she said grimly.

Jenna looked almost as amazed as I felt. "Are you serious?" she asked Claudia. "You'd really go out for the boys' team?"

"Sure." Claudia tossed her a wicked grin. "Want to do it with me?"

Jenna hesitated. I hoped it was because she was trying to figure out the best way to talk Claudia out of her insane idea. I certainly didn't want to be the one to do it.

"I don't think so," Jenna said at last, her voice unusually soft and tentative. "I—I don't think I'm up for that. Anyway, I kind of like field hockey. It won't be so bad."

"Suit yourself." Claudia's voice was brisk and businesslike, though I thought I caught a flash of disappointment on her face. "You'd better come cheer me on at my games, though."

"Deal," Jenna agreed immediately.

I had to put a stop to this before it went any further. Claudia obviously wasn't thinking straight. She wasn't really considering how her plan would turn out if she went through with it. But I was. I knew the guys on the soccer team—if she even showed up for the first day of tryouts that afternoon, they would hassle her mercilessly about it for the rest of her life.

Not just her, I added grimly to myself. *Me too. They'll probably start calling us Jock and Jill—and I won't be the one they're calling Jock.*

I opened my mouth to try to explain that to her. But the bell rang, cutting me off before I could begin.

"Ugh," Claudia said with disgust. "I haven't even picked up my schedule yet. We'll have to figure this out later."

Yeah, later, I thought with relief. I would have

to put off my little talk with Claudia until lunchtime. At least that meant I would have a few hours to figure out what to say.

By the time lunch hour rolled around, I'd almost convinced myself that I was all worked up for nothing. Claudia didn't always think things through before she spoke. I told myself that once she'd had a chance to calm down, to consider her options, she would realize how ridiculous her plan was. At least I hoped so. All morning long my overactive imagination had come up with all sorts of horrible scenarios for what would happen if she showed up at tryouts that afternoon. Joel Wyman would probably start leaving feminine hygiene products in my gym locker. Rude song lyrics were Rich Tarvell's specialty. Our goalie, Jason Kent, wasn't quite so creative. He would just take every opportunity to kick the ball directly at my crotch. Then there were the giggles and stares and obnoxious comments that would follow me everywhere I went after the news was out. Our school wasn't tiny, but it wasn't huge either. If Claudia came to tryouts, everyone would know by the end of homeroom the next morning. Everyone.

I stopped at my locker to drop off my books, then wandered down the hall, dawdling as I tried to convince myself that everything was going to be fine. I had almost reached the cafeteria door, lost in thought, when I heard heavy footsteps coming up fast behind me.

"Yo, A-man! What's up, little bro?" Bruce passed me at a swift jog, then doubled back and slammed into me playfully with one broad, beefy shoulder.

I did my best to hide my wince of pain at the impact. The way my brother treated me sometimes, it was hard to believe we were barely more than a year apart in age. I'd always had a hard time relating to him in any kind of normal brother-to-brother way, or even any human-to-human way. Still, I was a glutton for punishment. I never stopped thinking our relationship could be more normal if I could just figure out the right way to act around him.

"Nothing major," I told him casually. "I was, uh, just thinking about something Claudia said this morning."

"Let me guess. She's being difficult." Bruce rolled his eyes. "Huge surprise there."

I forced myself to smile blandly, mentally kicking myself for bringing up her name. Bruce and Claudia had never gotten along very well.

Bruce shook his head sadly. "You shouldn't let her ride you like she does," he said. "You've got to be a man. Take control of the situation."

Coming from anyone else, I would have thought a comment like that was a total joke. But I knew that Bruce meant every word. He didn't believe in long-term relationships or in letting a girl get the upper hand—ever. He'd dated a whole series of girls in his first three years of high school, and that pattern didn't seem likely to change anytime soon.

Bruce wasn't finished. He reached out and tapped me on the chest. "Or better yet, just ditch her. It's a new year—so find yourself a new girl. A *real* girl."

I didn't bother trying to explain to him what was wrong with that last statement. I could only imagine what he'd do to me if I looked him in the eye and said, *Claudia is more of a real girl, and a real* person, *than any twelve of your girlfriends put together. Besides that, I love her more than I ever thought I could love anyone—and I wouldn't trade her for all the cheerleaders in China.*

I paused long enough to wonder if they actually had cheerleaders in China, and I guess in the meantime Bruce got bored with the conversation. Several of his football buddies appeared, headed toward the cafeteria.

"Yo! Wait up!" he shouted at the top of his lungs, racing over to join them without a backward glance at me.

I watched him go, rubbing my sore shoulder. When it came to anything but football, Bruce had the attention span of a gnat, and this time I guessed it was just as well. I had to get to lunch and find out if Claudia had come to her senses.

I didn't see her on my way into the already-crowded cafeteria, but she was sitting at our table when I emerged from the lunch line. None of our other friends had turned up yet, and I approached her with a mixture of hope and dread. Looking at her familiar face—her gorgeous chocolate eyes, her thick, shiny hair—there was no way of telling what she had decided. I was dying to know.

Setting my tray down on the table, I glanced at her food. "Extra! Extra!" I joked. "Pigs fly in Randallstown! But now for our top story: Claudia Willoughby actually eats an egg roll. Can it be true?"

Claudia sniffed. "Very funny," she said, poking at the cylindrical object on the plate beside her tuna sandwich. "It came with the rest of the lunch, so I took it for you. I know you never turn down extra food, especially anything Chinese."

"True enough," I admitted, settling myself on the hard, round slab of wood the school called a seat and reaching over to snag the egg roll in question. "Thanks. I think my MSG levels are getting a little low. You know how dangerous that can be."

"Right," Claudia said with a snort. She hated Chinese food—in my opinion, her only serious flaw as a human being. I just hoped they would come up with a cure in our lifetimes so that I could someday share the ultimate intimacy with her—moo goo gai pan for two.

Claudia glanced up as Bruce strutted past our table with Lisa trailing in his wake. "I can't believe Bruce and airhead number forty-seven are still together," Claudia commented sarcastically. "That must be some kind of record. What is it—a month now?"

"Something like that." I was feeling tense, though I tried to hide it by stuffing one entire egg roll into my mouth at once. When I had chewed and swallowed and regained the power of speech, I decided it was time to take control of the situation, as Bruce would say. "Listen, Claud. Call me dense—"

"Okay, you're dense," she said immediately.

"—but I just wanted to double-check something," I plowed on, ignoring her predictable comment. "You were kidding about what you said this morning, right? I mean, about going out for the guys' team."

Her face darkened immediately. "What do you mean?" she demanded.

Uh-oh. She was already on the defensive, and I hadn't even gotten started yet. "Um, I was just wondering, that's all," I said weakly. "I mean, I was wondering if, you know, anyone would object or anything. I mean, if there are rules—if you would actually be allowed to—"

"I stopped by Coach Baker's office this morning after homeroom," Claudia said quickly. "He doesn't have a problem with my trying out for the team." She shot me a challenging glance. "Why? Do you?"

Definitely. Absolutely. With every beat of my heart.

"It's not that I have a problem with it," I said in my most reasonable tone. "It's just that I'm not sure you've really thought about what you're doing."

"Oh, really?" Her voice had suddenly gone ice-cold. That should have been a warning. So should the look she was giving me. It was a lovely little expression I had dubbed her spontaneous-combustion look, because it made her face seem as though it could explode at any second.

But like a fool, I plunged on.

"Yes," I told her. "Have you considered what people are going to say if you do this? Because I have, and it's not a pretty picture. They'll start calling you Xena and She-man and who knows what else."

She rolled her eyes. "Big deal," she said, ripping open her milk carton. "The only people's opinions *I* care about are those of the scouts from UNC looking for the next Mia Hamm."

"But have you considered the fact that they'll also be making fun of *me?*" I avoided her eyes. "I mean, how do you think it's going to look with both of us trying out for the same team?"

"I don't know. How *is* it going to look?"

She wasn't making this easy. "It's going to look bad. Real bad. The guys are going to ride me about it, and you know it."

She peeled the top piece of bread off her sandwich and carefully picked off the slimy, pinkish tomato slice from inside. "They'll get bored with that soon enough," she said matter-of-factly.

I decided it was time to switch tactics and appeal more directly to her feelings for the love of her life—as in me. "Think about this, then," I told her. "You play forward. I play forward."

"Right," she replied, glancing at me with a puzzled expression. "So?"

"That means if you go out for my—I mean the guys' team, we'll have to compete against each other. That can't be good for our relationship."

I kept my voice calm as I spoke, but inside I was beginning to feel a cold sense of desperation creep over me. Why couldn't Claudia understand what I was trying to tell her? Why didn't she care that her plan was going to put up a huge wall between us?

"There's more than one forward position on the team," she pointed out.

"I know, but—," I began helplessly.

"Besides," she interrupted, "our relationship should be strong enough to survive a little healthy competition." She shrugged. "So what's the big deal?"

We'd been together for a long time. But suddenly, staring me straight in the face, was the realization that in all that time, our relationship had never really been tested. Not like this. *Should that be telling me something?* I wondered uneasily, feeling my stomach flip. *If she won't even listen to me about this, how much can she really care about me? She's being totally unfair. We're a couple. Couples are supposed to stick together and think about each other's feelings. Doesn't she know that?*

"It's just—" I stopped, struggling to figure out how to explain this to her. "I mean, this was my team, you know?"

Claudia bit into her sandwich and started chewing. "But you're on *all* the teams," she argued through a mouthful of tuna. She paused, peering at me closely. "I know this really stinks for you," she acknowledged. I felt a wave of relief. So she *wasn't* just ignoring my words. "But how can I give up soccer? I've been dreaming about getting my first Olympic team medal since I was five!"

I sighed. She was right—soccer *was* much more important to her than it was to me. But somehow that wasn't even the point anymore. I needed to know that she could put me first for once, that my feelings mattered to her. And she was *still* talking as though being on the soccer team meant more than being with me!

"I understand that," I said in a softer tone. "I get what soccer is for you."

She smiled. "Good," she answered. "Then we're okay, right?"

I gritted my teeth at her words. Clearly she had made up her mind and had no intention of changing it or even considering the other side of the issue, no matter what I said. She'd never been so cold and rigid with me before, and it ticked me off in a big way. I was trying to be reasonable. I was trying to talk this out in a mature, open manner. But she just wanted me to shut up and let her do what she wanted.

I glanced up and saw Jenna and Sherry Collins heading toward us. Their arrival would cut this conversation short, so I knew I had only another minute. "Just promise you'll think about this—about what I said, okay?" I asked urgently.

She frowned, then nodded slowly.

I took a deep breath, then ripped my second egg roll in half. Now all I had to do was spend the rest of the day hoping that I wouldn't see Claudia on the field at tryouts that afternoon. Because if I did, then I'd know for sure how little I meant to her.

Three

Claudia

"HEY, GUYS!" JENNA dropped her lunch tray with a clatter on the table beside mine. "What's new?"

I glanced up and saw Sherry Collins was right behind her. I sighed, frustrated. "Nothing much," I lied with a sidelong glance at Aaron.

Sherry Collins, another member of our previous year's soccer team, took the seat beside me. "So, Willoughby," she said in her usual direct manner, reaching up to tighten her blond ponytail, "Jenna says you're thinking of going out for the guys' team. True?"

"I'm not sure yet," I lied again. I didn't want to get into it right then, not after what Aaron had said. I still couldn't believe that he really expected me to just drop my lifelong dream in order to make his existence a little less uncomfortable. Sure, the guys would tease him for a while, but was that really more important to him than my happiness? The whole thing had made me wonder just how much Aaron really cared about me.

As Jenna and Sherry started talking about their morning classes, I sneaked a quick peek at Aaron's face. He was bent over his lunch, his brows drawn together, his eyes trained on his food.

Maybe I should ask him if he wants to go someplace to finish talking, I thought. I mean, I could have misunderstood what he'd been trying to tell me, right? The idea that our relationship didn't mean as much to him as it did to me was too scary to take seriously.

I'd opened my mouth to ask him when we were interrupted by the arrival of a tall, lanky guy dressed in black jeans and a dark gray polo shirt.

"Peace, folks," Sam Wrightfield said as he tossed his long caramel-blond hair back over his angular shoulders. He was carrying a stack of papers and wearing a solemn expression. "Just wanted to let you know I'm holding a rally on Saturday to protest the hiring practices at the university. I hope you'll find time to come and support the hardworking minorities of this community."

I definitely wasn't in the mood for one of Sam's causes just then. Despite the fact that his mother was the local district attorney and his father owned half the town, Sam considered himself the last of the red-hot liberals, dedicated to lost causes and social justice. He was known as the Randallstown Radical.

"Do you mind, Sam?" I said irritably. "We're eating lunch here."

Sam hardly seemed aware of my rudeness. He dropped a handful of the papers from the stack he was holding onto my lunch tray, and several of them landed in my tossed salad. "Just take a look, okay?" he said. "Tell your friends. With everybody's help and support, we can ensure a fair work environment for all people." With that, he spun on the heel of one shiny black leather loafer and strode off to the next table.

I picked up one of his flyers, holding it gingerly by one corner and shaking off most of the salad dressing. Then I gave it a cursory glance. It was obviously fresh off the tray of Sam's color laser printer, and it featured the words *Stop Racism Now* in bold type across the top. Tossing the flyer aside, I returned my attention to Aaron.

What if he does care more about what the guys think than our relationship? a little voice inside my head piped up.

I shook my head, unwilling to consider that possibility. Aaron did understand how much soccer meant to me—he'd said so just a few minutes earlier. And once we were both out there on the field together at tryouts, I knew he'd support me and prove that being with me mattered more to him than all that other stuff.

I didn't have a chance to talk to Aaron all afternoon. We ended up in only two classes together, and with all the usual first-day-of-school frenzy, I just couldn't seem to catch him alone in the halls.

The girls' locker room was already crowded when I arrived, thanks to my last-period history teacher's refusal to accept that the bell meant his class was over. Several girls looked up and then away again quickly as I entered, which meant the news about my plan was out. I did my best to pretend not to notice the extra attention as I strode to my usual locker. Jenna was already sitting on the bench in front of it. "Hey," I greeted her, slinging my duffel onto the bench beside her and kicking off my shoes.

"Hey," she returned. She pulled a faded Redskins T-shirt over her head and shook out her curls, shooting me a curious glance. "So?" she began expectantly.

"I'm doing it," I declared.

She nodded and began to gather her hair into a thick, springy ponytail at the nape of her neck. "Cool."

I let out a breath I hadn't realized I was holding, and smiled. Having Jenna's support meant a lot.

"Good luck at field hockey tryouts," I told her as she swung her locker door shut.

"Thanks. You too. I mean, with the soccer team." She gave me one last encouraging smile, then turned and left.

I changed as quickly as I could before heading out toward the soccer field. Most of the guys who were trying out for the team were already gathered at one end of the field, talking or warming up by kicking a few balls around. Coach Baker was standing near the goal, examining something on his clipboard.

The coach looked up as I jogged toward the group. "Well, well, Willoughby," he said in his brisk, businesslike voice, his deep brown eyes twinkling. "So you meant what you said this morning. The field hockey team isn't getting all the leftovers from girls' soccer."

I didn't know Coach Baker very well, but I'd always liked him—he reminded me a little of my dad. It wasn't a physical resemblance—as a tall, rail-thin African-American with a bushy mustache, Coach Baker was the polar opposite of my dad when it came to looks. But both of them managed to keep their cool and their sense of humor while still remaining intensely competitive.

"Watch it," I joked. "Who're you calling a leftover?" I grinned at the coach and then turned to survey my competition.

That was when I first spotted Aaron. The gym shorts and T-shirt he had on revealed his muscular legs and broad shoulders. But that wasn't what stood out to me. It was the stunned expression on his face. He was staring at me—just flat-out staring, his jaw hanging down. When he saw that I'd noticed him, he snapped his mouth shut, scowled, and turned away.

I hurried over and grabbed him by the arm. "Hey," I said. "Listen, we should probably talk about this before tryouts get started."

"Look at the lovebirds," Joel Wyman sang out, jogging over to us with Jason Kent next to him.

"Hey, Aaron, shouldn't *you* be over at field hockey tryouts?" Jason chimed in.

Aaron's face was turning red, the way it did when a teacher called on him and he didn't know the right answer.

"Ignore them," I hissed through clenched teeth.

"Yeah, man, you'd better do what the lady says," Jason said tauntingly. "Sounds like she knows how to give an order."

Aaron winced. "There's nothing for us to talk about," he told me. His voice was eerily quiet, and the look in his eyes was unreadable.

I gulped. Aaron had never spoken to me that way before. Why couldn't he stand up to these guys for me? "Look," I said slowly, being careful to keep my temper under control. I realized uncomfortably that the rest of the team was gathering around us, watching the scene. "I already told you. This is something I have to do. You know how much soccer means to me."

Aaron's expression softened, and his eyes filled with confusion. *Finally I'm getting through to him,* I thought with relief.

"Looks like we've lost him now," Joel said, letting out a low whistle. "Give it up, Aaron," he called out.

I spun around. "We don't need you to tell us what to do," I spat out angrily. "Aaron doesn't care what you say." I turned back to Aaron. "Right?" I asked him.

"Save your breath, Claudia," Aaron said loudly. "You don't care what I think anyway."

I sucked in my breath, shocked by the coldness of his response. A couple of guys on the field nearby hooted appreciatively, and even more turned to see what was going on. I ignored them. My fists were clenched, but despite that, I felt my hands start to shake.

"Aaron," I began, "what's your problem? You know that I—"

"You heard him, babe," Jason said. "He doesn't want to follow any of your *commands*." I wasn't surprised that he was leading the group in stupid insults. Jason had a twenty-four-inch neck and an IQ to match. He was a pretty good goalie, though—mostly because he wasn't afraid to crash into the ground or goalpost headfirst if necessary.

I glared at him. "Get a clue, Kent," I snapped.

"Here's a clue for you, Willoughby." Joel spoke up from beside Jason. "Field hockey tryouts are on the south field. You must be lost."

I glanced at Aaron, desperate to see some sign of support from him. But he looked as disgusted as the rest of the guys, and he wouldn't even meet my eye.

"Joel's right," he said, his voice so low that for a moment I wasn't sure I was hearing him right. "Field hockey's on the south field. And—" He stopped, inhaling deeply. "And if you stick around here, we're through," he finished flatly.

I felt as though I'd been slapped. All the air left my body.

"What are you talking about?" I almost whispered.

Aaron's stony expression didn't change. "Need me to repeat it? Fine. If you try out for the soccer team, our relationship is over."

I swallowed, fighting back all the pain that his words sent through me. If he could even give me such a ridiculous ultimatum, then I couldn't let him see how much losing him hurt me.

"Fine," I said coldly. "Don't bother to talk to me again. Ever."

He put his hands on his hips. "I wasn't planning to."

"Get out of my way," I muttered, pushing my way past him and the other guys, most of whom were grinning and cheering at Aaron's response. I couldn't stand to listen to another word. And I definitely couldn't stand to spend one more second looking into the hostile face of the guy I'd thought I was in love with—the guy I'd thought was in love with me.

Luckily, they let me go. I didn't bother to look back, but I could tell I was alone as I jogged toward an abandoned black-and-white ball near the edge of the penalty area a dozen yards away. As soon as I felt the smooth, solid surface of the ball between my feet, I felt a tiny bit better, or at least more in control. I dribbled idly across the field, trying to make sense of what had just happened.

I couldn't believe Aaron was ready to dump me at the first sign of conflict, that he would resent me for going after what I wanted. I'd always thought he was so different from most guys—guys like his brother, sexist jerks who let their egos guide their every move.

I can't believe he'd do this to me, I thought. The pain was so overwhelming I could barely breathe. But I had to stay focused.

Turning toward the goal at the far end of the field, I broke into a sprint, still dribbling. *Concentrate on the ball,* I told myself, blocking out everything else. As I steadied and took a shot, sending the ball whizzing into the net, I heard the coach blow his whistle. It was time for tryouts to start, and I was ready.

Four

Aaron

"YO, HAYES!" JOEL Wyman shouted as he jogged past me down the field. We were scrimmaging in small groups, and it was my turn to watch from the sidelines. "Check out your girlfriend's action. Shouldn't you be making like a cheerleader and doing splits or something?"

I gritted my teeth and ignored him, trying not to notice as Claudia drove for the goal despite a slamming—not to mention illegal—body check from a sophomore named Anthony Pella, who was guarding her. Her shot was accurate and clean, burning air right past the tips of Jason's outstretched hands and whooshing cleanly into the back of the net.

Nobody said a word as Jason scrambled to retrieve the ball from the net and Claudia jogged back into position with the others, looking pleased with herself.

Her eyes were sparkling, and her whole face and body seemed alive with energy. She hardly seemed to notice the dirty looks she was getting from most of the guys—she was too wrapped up in her own play. As I watched, the reality of what I'd done finally sank into my thick head. I'd broken up with Claudia.

"I don't know, Hayes." Rich Tarvell strolled over to me, a smirk on his thin, pale face, as the coach yelled for a time-out and went out to talk to the players on the field. "Claudia looks pretty good out there. And I'm not just talking about her legs."

"Shut up, Tarvell," I muttered automatically. "You're just jealous because she's more of a man than you'll ever be."

Rich grinned delightedly, and I knew I'd chosen exactly the wrong insult. "Oh, yeah?" he hooted. "So let me get this straight . . ."

I sighed, preparing myself for the inevitable string of Aaron-dated-a-man jokes. Despite the fact that, as of an hour before, Claudia and I were no longer a couple, I knew the guys weren't going to let up on me anytime soon. *No longer a couple.* The words jumped out at me from my own thoughts. Claudia and I were over. It was totally incomprehensible, but it was real.

I thought about all the times that Bruce had lectured me: *Be a man, bro. Take control of the situation.* He'd warned me that it was wrong never to stand up to Claudia, because she'd think she could always do whatever she wanted.

Maybe he was right. Even with the guys hassling

me like that, Claudia hadn't cared how I felt. She hadn't even given me a chance to respond to them myself; she'd just turned around and acted as though she could think—and speak—for me. So I knew that for once I couldn't just sit back and let Claudia have her way. For one thing, it would prove to my teammates, my brother, and the world that I was the world's biggest wuss. More important, if I backed down, it would mean giving up all chance of an equal relationship, of self-respect, of ever knowing just how much she really cared when push came to shove. . . .

And now I knew the answer. She didn't.

"Whoa," Anthony murmured under his breath, just loud enough for me to overhear. "Nice move."

Turning to see what he was looking at, I saw that Claudia had the ball again and had just hustled it right past both Joel and Rich, who were chasing her down the field as she drove again for the goal.

"Stop her!" Jason bellowed, weaving back and forth in front of the net as he tried to anticipate which way she'd move. When she took her shot, he leaped forward just in time, deflecting the ball off his hand. Still, when I glanced at the coach, I saw that he was nodding approvingly, looking impressed.

My heart sank. Claudia was a killer on the field. She'd been far and away the best player on the girls' team the previous year, and she was more than holding her own against the guys in tryouts.

"Okay, listen up, men," Coach Baker called, clapping his hands for attention. Suddenly remembering Claudia, he shot her a guilty look. "Uh, I mean, listen up, *people*. I think that's enough for today. I want you all to show up here again tomorrow, same time, same place. Now go home and get some rest."

I turned and headed off the field, carefully avoiding looking in Claudia's direction.

Tryouts lasted three days, as usual. But I don't think three days have ever lasted longer. It was a strain to keep ignoring Claudia. Even though I was still angry, I cringed every time someone crashed into her on purpose or kicked the ball a little too hard on a pass. And I had to make a real effort to keep from telling Joel Wyman what a butthead he was after he tripped her when we were all running laps, sending her face-first into the muddy ditch between the field and the bleachers.

Worst of all, though, was the way Claudia looked straight through me whenever we faced each other, on the field or off, as if I were the Invisible Man. Or rather, the Invisible Man with BO. I couldn't believe she was being so stubborn. Was she really just going to act as though we'd never been more to each other than strangers? Or—I could barely even think it—did she just not miss me at all?

No, she was probably just still steamed about the breakup scene at tryouts. I was starting to feel kind of bad about the way it had happened. Soccer did mean more to Claudia than it did to me—I knew that. I'd broken up with her because she wasn't listening to how I felt, but shouldn't I have told her that directly?

On Wednesday, the third day of tryouts, I decided to do something. Maybe now that the pressures of tryouts would be over, we could get together and talk, work things out somehow.

I was sitting in front of my locker pulling on my cleats when Rich sat down on the bench next to me. "It's the moment of truth, Hayes," he said. "Soon we'll find out who's more of a man—you or Claudia."

"Very funny," I muttered. Part of me wanted to leap to Claudia's defense, but I knew better than that. The best thing was just to ignore all the comments and pretend they didn't bother me.

Rich leaned closer and grinned. "Hey, I don't blame you for being worried," he said. "She's pretty good—for a girl."

I shot him an angry look, sick of his stupid little digs. "I'm not worried," I said a little too loudly. "I made first string last year, remember?"

"Whatever," Rich drawled, standing up. "See you on the field. May the best man win." He put a little extra emphasis on the word *man,* and I winced. Why did I let that kind of garbage get to me? I was going to have to be stronger if I wanted to straighten things out with Claudia once tryouts were over.

Coach Baker worked us so hard that day that I almost managed to forget my problems. We all hustled our butts off the whole time. More than forty guys—and one girl—had showed up for each day of tryouts. Twenty of us, at best, would make varsity, and of those, only eleven would win spots on the starting team. I was pretty confident about my chances, as I'd told Rich, but I still wasn't about to let up on myself until it was all over.

Toward the end of the afternoon the coach set up another scrimmage, shirts versus skins. That brought out a few comments aimed in Claudia's direction, naturally, but the coach ignored them, quickly assigning her to be a striker on the shirts. I ended up defending for the skins.

"I want to see some hustle out there, people," Coach Baker barked as I peeled off my sweat-soaked T-shirt and flexed my tired shoulders. "This is your last chance to show me what you've got, so make it count."

"Right," Joel called out, flinging aside his own T-shirt and clapping his hands briskly. "This is where we separate the men from the boys."

The coach glanced at Claudia briefly, then shot Joel a stern look. But he didn't say anything. He just waved his arms to send us jogging into position.

For the first few minutes I didn't see much action. The forwards on my team got control of the ball early and kept it, expertly passing it back and forth among themselves, obviously grandstanding for the benefit of the coach. I couldn't help being impressed with some of the fancy footwork, though I was impatient to get my feet on the ball. If I wanted to lock in my spot on the starting team, this was the time to do it.

Finally one of the guys took a shot, sending the ball sailing easily past the freshman who was playing goalie for the shirts. When the ball came back in play, a shirt defender grabbed it and sent it to one of his midfielders with one swift, sure kick. The midfielder passed to a forward—not Claudia, I noted, though she had been closest—and I tensed, feeling adrenaline pound through my veins, reviving my tired legs as I jumped forward, ready to intercept.

The forward raced toward me, a look of determination on his face. He was concentrating so hard on controlling the ball that I guess he lost control of his feet. His shoe caught on a rough patch of grass, and he went down hard, landing half on the ball and sending it flying up and out at a wild angle.

Joel was playing midfield on my team, and he was ready. He leaped forward to meet the ball, catching it on his chest and bouncing it expertly in front of him. Yelling with excitement, he raced after the ball and started dribbling back down the field.

But he wasn't counting on Claudia. She'd been caught just a few yards behind him on the steal, and now she flew toward him and intercepted, executing a breathtaking slide tackle. Joel looked like a cat who'd just lost his tasty mouse dinner to a passing hawk.

Normally I might have enjoyed the spectacle. But now I realized that Claudia was pounding toward me, her face full of furious concentration and the ball zinging back and forth between her feet as she ran.

I hardly had time to breathe before she reached me. We'd played out this same scenario dozens, maybe hundreds of times in her yard, but never with such intense stakes. I could see the determined set of her jaw as she darted back and forth, trying to find a safe path around me.

Claudia feinted right and then drove left, but I was ready for her. I leaped for the ball, coming within a hairbreadth of snagging it. But at just the right second she dodged to the right again, then steamrolled past me before I knew what was happening. I tried to throw my body in front of her to block her, only it was too late. Her shoulder crashed into mine so hard my whole arm went numb for a second, but it didn't even slow her down. A moment later I heard her familiar whoop of triumph as she sent the ball zooming into the goal.

"Score!" the coach yelled. "Nice shot, Willoughby."

The scrimmage continued for a few more minutes, but all I could hear was the pounding in my own head, sounding strangely like my brother's voice shouting, *Beaten by a girl! Beaten by a girl!* over and over again. I did my best to ignore it, telling myself that it wasn't a big deal. But it was kind of hard to believe that when the other guys kept shooting me looks and snickering.

Finally the coach called for a halt. "Okay, folks," he announced. "It's time for me to put you out of your misery. Gather around."

We were all so wrung out that we looked like war survivors as we shuffled over to where the coach was standing. I wondered if my face was as pale and nervous as most of the other guys'. For once, nobody was paying any attention to Claudia as she mopped her brow and stared at the coach. Everyone was too busy crossing their fingers and waiting to hear their fate.

Coach Baker didn't keep us in suspense for long. "I had a tough time making my decisions this year," he told us, tugging at his mustache and consulting his clipboard. "You should all be proud of your effort. To prove the point, I'm not cutting anyone—you'll all have a place on one of the teams. Now, here's the JV starting lineup. . . ."

I zoned out a little at that point, hardly taking in the list of junior-varsity players, mostly freshmen. My gaze kept wandering to Claudia. Her hair was plastered to her head by sweat, her shirt was sopping wet and clinging to her body, her legs were covered with grass stains and dirt. But all I wanted was to hold her.

"Hit the showers, JV players," the coach ordered after he'd read the list. As the younger players headed off toward the gym, he flipped to the second page on his clipboard and nodded. "All right, then. Varsity. Here's our starting team. In the goal once again, we'll have Mr. Kent."

Jason pumped his fist in the air. "All right!" he shouted.

Coach Baker smiled, then continued. "Our three defenders will be Mr. Tarvell . . ."

I tuned him out again, feeling the tension well up in me as he read off the list of defenders and midfielders. I glanced at Claudia. She still looked tired, but if she was nervous, nobody ever would have guessed it. Her expression was calm, almost serene. I'd seen it before, usually in situations like this, when she was relaxing in the face of pressure. I called it her Zen goddess face.

"Good luck, Hayes," Charlie Donnelly whispered. Charlie had been one of my fellow forwards on the team the previous year, and he was a decent guy, quiet and thoughtful.

I shot him a quick grin to show that I wasn't worried. "You too, man," I murmured. "Hope we both make it."

"And now," the coach said, "in the forward position, we have the following three players." He glanced down at his clipboard once more. "Mr. Donnelly."

Okay, Charlie was in. Now there were two spots left. Two spots that could be filled by—

"Mr. Wyman."

Joel. That meant it was down to me and Claudia. I couldn't believe it—this was *exactly* what I'd been afraid of. Competing against my own girlfriend. Only one of us would—

"And Ms. Willoughby."

I could have sworn my heart stopped dead for a good ten seconds. By the time it started again, the surprised murmurs had reached a crescendo.

"Hey, Coach," Jason Kent called out, sounding angry. "Is this some kind of joke? It's bad enough you let her"—he jerked a thumb in Claudia's direction—"try out in the first place. You can't actually expect us to play with a girl on the starting team."

Coach Baker stared Jason down, folding his arms across his chest. "I do expect it, Mr. Kent," he said evenly. "If you've got a problem with the way I've assigned the positions, you're just going to have to deal with it. I don't expect to hear about it again. Understood?"

There were a few more surly murmurs. I kept quiet, knowing that my face was burning right down to my earlobes, wondering exactly what the chances were that a meteor would plummet to earth and destroy us all in the next few seconds. Claudia had taken my position. It was too awful to be real.

Joel Wyman stepped forward to stand beside Jason. "What if he's not the only one who has a problem with it?" he asked in his most threatening voice. When Joel talked like that, most people backed down. Even teachers had been known to shudder under his steady, chilling gaze.

But the coach didn't flinch. "Same goes," he replied, his voice just as cool as Joel's. He glanced around at the group. "I realize this situation is a bit unusual, but the bottom line is that Claudia earned her place on the team as fairly as anyone else, and that's all I care about. My job is to coach you all to be the best players you can be. I'm not paid to coach you through any personal problems you may have with each other, and I'm not going to do it. That sort of garbage is a waste of my time, and of yours, and it won't help us win any games. Am I making myself clear?"

Joel and Jason kept quiet, but they didn't look happy. The coach paused for a few seconds, as if daring them to speak up. Finally he nodded, seeming satisfied.

"Now, as I said, I don't expect to hear another

word on this topic." He tucked his clipboard under one arm. "Anyone whose name I didn't call just now is on backup. That doesn't mean you get off easy. I expect everyone on my team to work, second string just as hard as the first. Got it? Then get out of here, all of you. Take a day off. I'll see you at practice on Friday right after school."

He turned away and strode toward the school building. As the rest of us followed more slowly, Joel caught up to me. "This is your fault, Hayes," he hissed. "If you'd kept the little woman in line and convinced her to try out for field hockey like she was supposed to, this team wouldn't be about to become the joke of the county."

Jason joined us just in time to hear what Joel said. "No kidding," he added, shrugging his heavy shoulders. "But what can we expect from Hayes? He couldn't even stop her when she stole the ball that time." He chortled. "She drove right past him like he was sitting around having a tea party with his dollies. No wonder he's stuck being a benchwarmer while She-man is a starter."

As I felt my face flush an even deeper shade of red, I considered reminding him that Claudia had gotten several shots past him when he was in the goal that day, but these guys weren't looking for logic. They just wanted to humiliate someone, and they'd obviously decided I was an easier target than Claudia.

I could play the macho game as well as anyone, though—hadn't I spent sixteen and a half years living with my brother? "Get real, Kent," I drawled as casually as I could manage. "I could have taken the ball from her anytime I wanted."

"Right," Joel said sarcastically. "Sure you could have."

I shrugged, determined to keep up the act. I might have lost my starting position, but that didn't mean I had to lose every last scrap of dignity too. "Who knew it would backfire like this?" I said, kicking at the grass as I walked. "I mean, I just let her win out on that play because I didn't want to make her cry or anything—after all, she's just a girl."

I glanced over at Jason, but he wasn't looking at me. He was smirking at someone I couldn't see on his other side. I quickened my pace and then felt my stomach cave, as though I'd just been kicked.

Claudia.

She was staring at me with her mouth hanging open. Right away I knew she'd heard every word I'd just said. Her expression wavered between pain, anger, and confusion before settling on anger.

"Claudia . . . ," I began, totally clueless about what to say. How could I have hurt her like that?

Five

Claudia

"DON'T DO ME any favors, Hayes," I snapped. "You couldn't have stolen that ball from me on your best day and my worst."

I didn't stick around to wait for him to come up with a response. I felt hot tears pricking my eyelids, and I wasn't about to let him—or his loser friends—have the satisfaction of seeing me cry. I jogged off toward the locker room, hardly pausing to give the coach a quick wave of thanks as I passed him and he called out, "Nice hustle out there today, Claudia."

I slowed to a walk when I was a safe distance from the others, taking a few deep breaths to get my emotions back under control. Even after everything that had happened, I never would have believed that Aaron could be such a total and complete jerk.

Most of all, I couldn't believe I'd wanted to apologize—that was why I'd caught up with him. I'd felt awful that he hadn't made the starting team. Soccer wasn't Aaron's life the way it was mine, but sports were still pretty important to him. Losing the position had to sting, and as mad as I was at him for not understanding what I needed to do, I hated to see him hurt and humiliated in front of everyone.

At least that was how I'd felt until I heard Aaron trashing me behind my back to those two jerks thirty seconds earlier and discovered what kind of person he really was.

"If that's the way you want it, fine with me," I muttered under my breath. I felt the burning sensation behind my eyelids again, but once more I fought back the tears, knowing Aaron could catch up to me at any moment. Whatever I did, I couldn't let him see how much he'd hurt me.

"Thank God it's Friday," Jenna moaned as she slammed the door of her little red two-door car and slung her patent-leather backpack over one bare shoulder. She was wearing a spaghetti-strap purple tank top, cut low in the back to show off her tattoo. "I couldn't survive another day. I'm not even sure I'm going to make it through today."

I smiled thinly as we started off through the student parking lot. "How do you think I feel?" I asked. "At least when you walk into a room, people don't stare at you as though you just sprouted a second head."

"My English teacher does," Jenna countered with a sly grin. "Anyway, I still think it's cool that you're a school celebrity. You should enjoy it."

I grimaced. "Easy for you to say. Three-quarters of the population of Randallstown High doesn't hate your guts."

"Hey, Claudia!" someone yelled. "You rule!"

I smiled weakly at the clutch of freshman girls from which the comment had originated. I had no idea which of them had spoken, and I didn't really care. They all looked the same anyway, with their matching soft-goth outfits, raccoon eyeliner, and cautiously rebellious attitudes.

"See what I mean?" Jenna said with a smirk. "Plenty of people think you're great. I should probably cash in on this trend and start a Claudia Willoughby fan club. I could sell copies of your elementary-school pictures, give tours of your neighborhood. . . ."

"Stop." I gave her a friendly shove.

Plenty of people think I'm great—except, of course, for Aaron, the one who matters. . . .

We reached the school steps, where the football team, the cheerleaders, and their hangers-on always hung out before school, flirting and giggling and generally being obnoxious. As we passed them all conversation stopped. I could feel their gaze upon me like wolves' eyes following a newborn lamb.

I shook off that image, doing my best to act normal and carefree as Jenna and I hurried up the steps and entered the school. I relaxed a little once we were inside.

"Now do you get it?" I asked. "Believe me, it's no fun getting major hostility vibes from all sides wherever you go."

"It's not from all sides." Jenna nodded toward a couple of guys who were watching us from the doorway of the computer lab. When they saw they'd been noticed, they quickly ducked inside again. "A lot of people think what you're doing is cool, even if they don't say so. And it's not just computer nerds who see you as Xena and Tank Girl all rolled up into one."

I grimaced. "Gee, thanks."

"It's true," she insisted. "Sure, a few blockhead jocks and their big-haired girlfriends think you're evil incarnate. If you ask me, you should take it as a compliment. Besides, a lot more people think you're some kind of girl-power goddess."

She had a point. My former teammates from the girls' soccer team, along with a lot of other athletic-type girls, had come up to me over the past few days to tell me that they supported what I was doing. So had some of the more independent-minded non-jocks, male and female.

"Okay, so maybe only *half* the student body hates me," I said, trying not to think about the one member of that half who was the reason I'd cried myself to sleep all week. I grinned weakly as we turned the corner into the hall where our lockers were located. "And as long as I'm still *your* hero . . ."

"You know it, girl," Jenna replied promptly. "I'm all for your going after what you want, you know that." She hesitated and gave me a quick sidelong glance.

"What?" I prompted, sensing she had something else to say.

She cleared her throat and shrugged. "I just wish . . . Never mind."

"What?" I asked again, worried that I knew exactly where she was going with this. "What do you wish?"

"It's nothing," she insisted. "I still just think it's too bad you and Aaron . . . Well, you know."

It wasn't the first time she'd brought up Aaron's name in the past couple of days. I was getting sick of explaining that I didn't want to discuss him, even with my best friend. The only way I could keep from bursting into tears right there in school was to force the knowledge that Aaron even existed as far out of my consciousness as possible.

"Look, I know you're sick of hearing it," Jenna continued more forcefully. "It's just that you guys always seemed so great together. I was convinced he was good for you, you know?"

"No, I don't know," I said, gulping. "How exactly is a stupid, macho, insensitive, lying jerk good for me?"

"I just think it's a shame, that's all," Jenna answered with a shrug.

I'd told her all the details of the breakup, but I was starting to think she'd missed a beat somewhere. "You almost sound like you think it was a mistake to break up with him," I challenged her, ignoring the fact that I'd wondered the same thing over and over myself. "Are you forgetting that pathetic ultimatum? What was I supposed to do?"

We'd reached her locker by now, and she dropped her bag on the floor and started to twirl the combination lock expertly. "No, you're right," she said thoughtfully. "That ultimatum was a really bad move. You did what you had to do, I guess."

"Okay, then," I said. I felt an empty satisfaction at finally having convinced her. "I'd better get to my locker. See you in third period."

Jenna groaned. "Ugh, don't remind me. I spent hours struggling over those chem problems last night. Is it possible to flunk out of a class in the first week?"

I grinned. "Later." I left her moaning into her locker over her academic performance and headed down the hall to my own locker. After dumping my bag and grabbing a few books, I continued on to homeroom.

Sam Wrightfield was lounging against the wall outside the classroom, looking as sleek and well-groomed as he usually did. I shot him a puzzled glance, wondering why he hadn't gone into homeroom yet.

He looked up just in time to catch my curious expression. I blushed. "Um, hi," I said, preparing to walk past him into the room.

But he straightened up quickly and reached out to put a hand on my arm. "Claudia," he said. "I was waiting for you."

"You were?" I said cautiously, wondering if my new teammates had hired him to lead a protest against me. "Uh, well, here I am." I looked down at my arm uncertainly, noticing that he hadn't let go.

He smiled broadly, as if what I'd said had actually been witty. "I know we don't know each other very well, Claudia . . . ," he began.

That was an understatement. Sam and I traveled in totally different circles. In his spare time, he was much more likely to attend a poetry reading or hang out at the library reading philosophy than catch the Redskins game on TV.

". . . and I hope you don't mind my approaching you like this," he continued, "but I just wanted to tell you how much I admire you for the stand you're taking by joining the men's soccer team."

"Thanks. It's not a big deal, really. I just wanted to play."

"It *is* a big deal, Claudia. One might say you're the ultimate feminist, holding her own in a male-dominated world." He moved his hand a little higher on my arm and squeezed gently before letting his arm drop to his side again. "I have to tell you, I find that very admirable."

"Thanks," I said again. I wasn't sure what else to say. His level gaze was making me a little nervous.

"I was just wondering if you were planning on coming tomorrow. To my protest, I mean. You know, at the university. I thought we might have dinner afterward if you're free."

"Um . . ." I didn't want to admit that I'd barely glanced at his flyer, let alone thought about what it meant. "The protest. Right."

If Sam noticed my cluelessness, he didn't let on. "It should be very exciting. Did you know there are only three minority professors in the entire university engineering department, and only two in the history department? Most of the other departments are almost as bad. We can't let this atrocity continue—I want to make sure the voices of hardworking minority academics are heard so that they have a fair chance at the best jobs in their fields."

"Sounds like a good cause," I said lamely.

He leaned a little closer and smiled. His teeth were white and even, and I noticed he had a small dimple in one cheek. It gave his perfectly symmetrical, high-cheekboned face just the right human touch. "So how about it?" he asked. "Will you let me take you to dinner after the protest? I'd really like to get to know you better."

My first instinct was to say no, I had a boyfriend.

But then I remembered that I *didn't* have a

boyfriend. Not anymore. Aaron and I were history, and that meant there was no reason in the world I shouldn't go out with someone else. Especially someone smart and good-looking, like Sam Wrightfield. Someone who was interested in me *because* of my devotion to soccer rather than being threatened by it.

Taking a deep breath, I cracked a smile. "Thanks," I told Sam. "I'd really like that. What time does the protest start?"

I almost missed his answer. I was too busy picturing the look on Aaron's face when he found out how totally over him I was. I couldn't wait to see it.

Six

Aaron

WHOEVER SAID TIME heals all wounds was full of it. It was already Friday and I still felt just as horrible about losing Claudia as I had in the first thirty seconds after we broke up. Of course, I felt pretty lousy about losing my spot on the starting team too, but that was manageable. Staying apart from the girl I loved was just too hard. There wasn't enough time in the world to heal that horrible, gaping wound.

It's almost lunchtime, I thought, glancing at the clock on the wall of my trigonometry classroom. *Maybe I should try to talk to her then.* I chewed my lower lip thoughtfully. *Then again, maybe I'd be better off waiting for a moment when I don't have an audience. I don't seem to do too well when other people are listening.* I winced as

I remembered that idiotic story I'd told Jason and Joel.

I was still worrying about it when the bell rang, releasing me from the frying pan of trig and into the fire of lunch period. My feet carried me automatically toward the cafeteria. Halfway there I spotted Jenna standing at her locker talking to Sherry. That gave me an idea. The girls' backs were to me, and I turned and approached them hesitantly. Jenna and I had always gotten along pretty well, but I knew how that best-girlfriend thing worked. If Claudia was mad at me, Jenna was probably mad at me too.

Don't be a wuss, I told myself firmly. *Just talk to her. Ask her what you should do about Claudia. She'll tell you the truth. She'll know if you have a shot at getting back together.*

I took a deep breath and another step toward Jenna. By now I was close enough to hear what she and Sherry were talking about.

". . . but I've always thought he was kind of cute," Sherry was saying. "I'm glad she decided to go for it."

Jenna ran a hand through her wild reddish curls. "I guess I am too," she said. "I mean, I never thought Claudia would be into someone like Sam—he's so serious and intellectual. But she seems psyched about their date tomorrow."

Their date tomorrow . . . The words hit me like a swift kick to the gut. I backed away quickly, almost tripping over my own feet in my haste to escape before the girls saw me. Once I was safely around a corner, I collapsed against the wall.

A date. Claudia had a date already, with *another guy*. I couldn't believe it. How could she be interested in that rent-a-rebel poseur Sam Wrightfield? But more important, how could she have gotten over our breakup so quickly?

"I guess I was right," I muttered to myself, feeling a heavy depression settle over me. Claudia really didn't care. She didn't miss me or need me or want me back. This breakup wasn't tearing her apart, as it was doing to me. My worst fear was coming true—Claudia hadn't listened to my feelings about the soccer team because *I didn't matter to her.*

I took a deep breath, trying to clear my mind as I started toward the cafeteria. But before I'd taken three steps, I knew it was a bad idea. My knees were shaking so hard I was afraid I'd topple over right there in front of everyone.

I grabbed a nearby water fountain for support, willing my body to behave. *Get a grip, Hayes,* I told myself sternly.

But I wasn't going to be able to tough this one out—I needed to be by myself for a few minutes. I needed to figure out how to go on breathing without Claudia in my life.

I glanced up and down the hall, searching for an escape. The computer lab was usually deserted at lunchtime, and it was just a few doors down from where I was standing. Keeping my head low, I shuffled toward the classroom, staring straight down at the floor.

"Hey!" a deep, familiar voice called out.

"Bruce?" I glanced up and saw my brother standing in front of me, actually appearing concerned.

"Aaron, bro!" Bruce said, running one large hand over his dark blond buzz. "What's going on?"

I backed up a few steps. "Nothing," I said. "I've got to—"

"Wait." Bruce moved closer to me. "You look kind of, I don't know, upset or something."

Why bother lying to him? "Actually, my life sucks," I replied. "Thanks for asking."

Bruce leaned back against the wall and folded his arms across his broad chest. "Is this about your jock ex?" he asked me.

I cringed. "Claudia and I are definitely over," I said dully. "She's already got a date with someone else this weekend. Obviously she was never really that into me after all."

Bruce seemed to be expecting something more. When he realized that I was done, he clapped me on the shoulder. "I never understood what you saw in Claudia anyway," he said cheerfully. "She's way too bossy. And now she's trying to become a guy on top of it all, going out for the team and everything. What you need is to get over your tomboy fixation and find out what it's like to be with a normal girl."

"You mean like Lisa?" My words were pretty sarcastic, but Bruce didn't seem to notice.

"Right. And I have just the girl for you. You know Lisa's friend Hilary?"

I nodded. Hilary Walters was on the cheerleading squad with Lisa. She was a senior, so I didn't know her too well. But I knew her by sight—she was hard to miss. She had wavy reddish blond hair, big blue eyes, and a body that would have stood out on *Baywatch*. Practically every guy in school started drooling whenever she walked by.

"I know her," I said casually.

Bruce grinned wickedly. "Well, you may get the chance to get to know her a lot better," he said. "She told Lisa she thinks you're cute." He smacked me gleefully on the shoulder. "Go figure, huh?"

I forced myself to laugh along as he chortled at his own joke. But inside I was practically fainting from astonishment. Hilary Walters—*the* Hilary Walters—thought I was cute? She'd actually said that?

"Anyway," Bruce continued, "I'm sure she'd say yes if you asked her out."

"Really?" I didn't want to go out with Hilary Walters—did I? Most guys would give up a kidney—*both* kidneys—for a shot at a date with her. But in my present state I wasn't the least bit interested in getting involved with a new girl. Even if I had been, I'd never been the type to lust after bimbos. I preferred brains along with beauty.

"Really," Bruce assured me. "And I think you should do it. You deserve a girl who appreciates you, bro." He clapped me on the shoulder again, and this time I hardly noticed the pain.

He could be right about that, I told myself. *Maybe he's not the most enlightened guy in the world when it comes to women, but this time he does have a point. I mean, why should I sit around pining after one girl when there's another one just dying to get to know me? It's not as if Claudia thought about me for more than two seconds before getting right back into the dating game. . . .*

"You know, Bruce, I think you're absolutely right." I stared at my brother thoughtfully. "I think I'll go find Hilary right now and see if she's free this weekend."

"That's my boy." Bruce grinned and gave me a thumbs-up. "Go for it."

I left the room and headed down the hall. I knew I'd have to work fast or I'd lose my nerve. Luckily, once I entered the cafeteria, Hilary wasn't hard to spot. She was perched on the edge of a table at the far side of the room, tossing her hair and laughing at something a girl sitting next to her was saying.

I wiped both palms on the front of my jeans and gulped a couple of lungfuls of Salisbury-steak-scented air. Then I started forward before I could change my mind. I was careful not to let the slightest thought of Claudia enter my head. I didn't want to get distracted.

Hilary spotted me when I was a couple of yards away. She looked surprised at first. Then she smiled. "Hi, Aaron."

Her girlfriend slipped away as I reached the table. I hardly noticed. I was staring, mesmerized by Hilary's beautiful blue eyes. Well, okay, maybe it wasn't just her eyes I was looking at—maybe I also noticed the smooth, soft skin just above the plunging neckline of her crop top. But her eyes were gorgeous too—the color of the ocean, fringed with long, dark lashes. Every inch of her was incredible.

"H-Hi," I managed to stutter out. "Um, hi."

Real smooth, Aaron, I told myself. *Snap out of it, or you're going to mess this one up too.*

Miraculously, Hilary was still smiling at me. She seemed to be waiting for me to say something.

I did my best. "Um, I was wondering," I tried again. What was the matter with me? Well, it had been a long time since I'd asked anyone out for a first date. Nine months, to be exact. "I mean, I was hoping you might want to get together this weekend. With me." She hadn't said anything yet. Suddenly I started to panic. "Uh, I realize it's short notice—if you're busy, I understand. I just—"

"No, no," she said at last. She was still smiling—another miracle. "It's okay, Aaron. I'd love to go out with you. How about tomorrow night? We could have dinner or something if you want."

"Great!" The feeling of relief that washed over me was so strong that it almost knocked me over. "Dinner would be great. I'm so glad you're free. And I really am sorry about the short notice."

"I understand." Hilary leaned forward and put a hand on my arm. I noticed that she smelled sweet, like flowers. Very feminine. "It's okay. The whole school knows what your ex put you through this week."

It took a moment for it to register that she was talking about Claudia. "Oh. Um . . ."

"Really, I understand, Aaron." Hilary slid off the table so that she was standing right in front of me. She was a little shorter than I would have expected—the top of her head only reached my chin, and I had to tilt my head down to look at her. Her hand was still resting lightly on my arm as she gazed up at me with those incredible eyes. "Maybe I shouldn't say so," she went on, "but personally, I can't believe Claudia could do something like that to someone she was supposed to care about."

I felt a jolt of pleasant surprise as I gazed down into her beautiful, earnest, totally sympathetic face. Could someone else actually understand what I was going through? I'd always assumed that Hilary was just one more beautiful airhead. But now I realized I might have judged her unfairly.

"Thanks," I told her, putting my hand over hers and squeezing. Suddenly all the misery and humiliation of the past week seemed a little less overwhelming.

Suddenly I couldn't wait for my date with Hilary.

Seven

Claudia

I TRUDGED ONTO the field for our first practice, eyeing my teammates warily. I had no idea what to expect, but I was prepared for the worst. I froze for a minute when I saw Aaron talking to Joel Wyman and a couple of other guys. The sight of him still made my whole body ache with sadness. I watched him for a second, waiting to see if he'd glance my way, but he just kept laughing with them, as if I weren't even there.

"Let's get started with some stretching," Coach Baker instructed once we were all on the field. "I'll take you through some basic stretches, and then we'll run a scrimmage."

I watched him demonstrate, and quickly recognized the stretch. I grabbed my foot and pulled my leg back like his, holding the ankle and staying steady on my other foot.

Suddenly someone bumped into me, knocking me off balance. I stumbled and almost fell, but managed to catch myself. I turned, annoyed, and saw Jason Kent smirking at me.

"Sorry," he said, looking anything but.

"That's enough," Coach Baker snapped, glaring at Jason. "Make sure there's enough space between you for those of you who are less *graceful* than others."

A couple of guys snickered, and I felt my cheeks redden, even though it hadn't been my fault. I sneaked a peek at Aaron, who was staring down at the ground.

Once we'd finished stretching, Coach Baker quickly divided us into scrimmage teams. I got into position with Joel and Charlie, the other forwards on my team. My blood heated up as I eagerly anticipated the action.

When the ball came our way, the midfielder passed it right to Joel. I dodged around the guy defending me, waving my arms to indicate that I was open and had a clear shot at the goal. But Joel ignored me, kicking the ball over to Charlie. Charlie sprinted forward, but not in time. The defender stole it easily, sending it flying back down the field.

"Wyman!" Coach Baker yelled out, blowing his whistle to stop play. "Willoughby was wide open. What's your problem?"

Joel shrugged. "I didn't think she'd get the pass," he said lamely.

I took a deep breath. So this was what I was in for.

It continued like that for a while. Every time

Joel had the ball, he'd pass it to anyone *except* me, even when I was obviously the most open person. Then one time Charlie actually dove for the ball and made it, staying free of the guy defending him. He still didn't have a good angle for a shot, though, and he turned, motioning for me to get ready for a pass. My muscles tightened as I waited for him to wing the ball over to me. As soon as I had it against my foot, I dribbled a little and kicked it hard toward the goal. It sailed past the goalie's outstretched hands and hit the back of the net.

"Yes!" I pumped my fist in the air, exhilarated from the satisfaction of a good play. Charlie smiled at me encouragingly, but the rest of the players didn't make a sound. I felt my energy deflate without their support. Part of the fun of scoring was the excitement that would always ignite the whole team. But I'd forgotten that these guys weren't going to share anything with me—not even the thrill of victory.

"All right, everyone, that's enough for today," Coach Baker called out. "Hit the locker room—uh, rooms."

I started walking back across the field, and I noticed Aaron and the coach talking about something together, looking serious. By the time I got to the bleachers, Aaron had left, but the coach waved me over to his side.

My eyes narrowed in confusion. Had Aaron been saying something to him about me?

"What's up?" I asked when I reached him.

"I'm concerned about the tension between you

and the guys on the team," he said, watching me closely. "If we're gonna win, we have to play *together*. I know the guys are giving you a hard time, and I just want to know if you're handling it okay."

I swallowed. Was I going to get cut just because a bunch of immature clods couldn't deal with playing with a girl? Then my hands went cold as another thought struck me: Had Aaron tried to convince the coach to cut me?

"I'm fine," I responded tightly.

He nodded. "Yeah, so far you seem to be," he acknowledged. "And you sure are a dynamo on the field."

I blushed at his compliment, relieved that he wasn't going to kick me off the team.

"Just let me know if the guys keep this up, okay?" he asked. "I'll try to figure out how to work the team through this."

"Thanks," I said, eager to end the conversation. "See you Monday, Coach."

He gave another brief nod, and then I turned and ran back to the school building.

Field hockey practice was still going, so I was the only one in the girls' locker room when I got there. I sank down onto the bench in front of my locker, then swung open the locker door to grab my clothes.

I blinked.

The locker was filled with dirty socks, and a big piece of paper on top of them had the words *Get off our team* scrawled across it. I sucked in my breath. They would sink this low? Then I flashed back to the image of Aaron talking to the coach, and a horrible fear crept over me. What if he'd told the coach to talk to me so that the guys would have time to do this, to leave me a little surprise? Could he do something so evil?

I didn't know. I didn't know *what* to think anymore, but obviously breaking up with Aaron had been the right thing to do.

"Equal rights, equal work!" I shouted at the top of my lungs. "Stop unfair hiring practices now!"

I waved around the handmade sign I was holding, which read Doesn't Everyone Deserve a Good Job? in rainbow letters. I'd never realized that protesting injustice could be so exhilarating. All around me, about a dozen other protesters were holding similar signs, shouting similar slogans. It was really a wild scene, like nothing I'd ever done before.

When we'd first arrived at the college green around lunchtime, a few university students and administrators had come out of the surrounding buildings to watch us. Most of that original audience had long since lost interest and wandered away, but as the afternoon wore on, new passersby kept stopping to check us out.

The sun was sinking lower in the sky, casting a rosy pinkish glow over the university buildings, when I noticed Sam approaching me. I shouted out a few more slogans as he continued toward me, noting at the same time how amazingly handsome he looked in his charcoal suede blazer and black jeans. The outfit seemed a little warm for September in

Virginia, but I was willing to let that slide. The dark colors of the fabric made his dark blond hair glow golden as the warm sun struck it.

"Hi," I said when he reached me.

"Hi," he returned, smiling as he gazed into my eyes. "I think the protest has been a big success—we've really gotten our message across to a lot of people. In fact, I think it's about time for us to wrap it up and get started on our dinner date. What do you say?"

I grinned and handed him the sign. "Let's do it," I said. "Today has been fun, but all this protesting is making me hungry."

One of the other protesters, a scraggly-looking college student, raced up to us. "Sam," he panted, "someone just spotted a TV news van heading this way."

Sam's eyes lit up. "Thanks, I'm on it," he told the student. Then he shot me an apologetic glance. "Sorry. But we can't pass up this chance to get more publicity for our cause. It shouldn't take long."

"No problem. My stomach can wait a few more minutes." I took back the sign and watched as he hurried off in the direction of the street. It was a breezy day, and the wind was blowing his hair all over the place as he ran. I smiled as I saw him try to smooth it back into place as he checked around for the news van.

Then he disappeared behind a hedge, and I turned away, leaning on my sign. The protest was winding down, and I realized that our real date was about to begin. It was a strange thought. I had trouble believing that I was actually out with a new guy, a guy who wasn't Aaron.

Aaron. The thought of him sent a wave of sadness through me so powerful I almost had to sit down. Why did it still hurt so much?

It's only natural, I rationalized. After all, Aaron and I had been together for so long. But then again, every good moment we'd spent with each other should have been canceled out by the way he'd acted in the past week. I stood up straighter as the pain was quickly replaced by burning anger. How could he have treated me like that? Obviously he wasn't who he'd seemed.

"Ready to go?" Sam's voice startled me out of my thoughts. Glancing up at his slightly flushed, smiling face, I realized that if anyone could distract me from obsessing over the breakup, it was Sam. He was so different, so interesting.

"I'm ready," I said quickly. "So how did the TV stuff go?"

"Great." He took my sign again and offered his other arm to me gallantly. "The reporter taped a short interview with me and promised to cover the protest on the ten o'clock news."

I took his arm and we strolled across the short-cropped grass of the college green to the sidewalk, where the other protesters were milling around, dropping their signs in a pile near someone's van and talking about the day's accomplishments. Sam added my sign to the pile, passed around a few words of thanks and congratulations, and then we made our exit.

Sam's black coupe was parked just down the

block, but instead of heading toward it, he led me off down the sidewalk in the opposite direction. "Where are we going?" I asked.

He glanced down at me. He was tall—a good two inches taller than Aaron—and I had to tilt my head back to meet his gaze. A small smile was playing around the corners of his mouth. "Well, I was going to keep it a surprise," he said. "But I don't have the heart to hold a beautiful woman in suspense. I've made reservations at Bonne Foi."

I wasn't sure whether to blush with pleasure at his compliment or gasp in amazement at his restaurant choice. Bonne Foi was the newest, trendiest, and most expensive restaurant in our little town. Most of my dates with Aaron had been pretty ordinary—movies, pizza in front of the ball game on TV, riding our bikes or hiking in the state park. For our six-month anniversary, he'd taken me up to Baltimore for a baseball game. Our dinner had consisted of hot dogs with lots of mustard, greasy stadium popcorn, and a jumbo soda with two straws. At the time it had felt perfect. But fancy restaurants were the *real* stuff of dream dates, right?

"How did you get us in there?" I blurted out, before realizing that it probably wasn't a very tactful question.

Sam didn't seem to mind. Pulling his arm in to bring me closer, he leaned toward me and winked mysteriously. "I have my ways," he murmured lightly. "I wanted to make sure this evening was special—special enough for a fascinating woman like you, Claudia."

This time I did blush. I wasn't sure how to respond. Sam sounded like a suave leading man in a movie—the things that came out of his mouth were hardly the usual high-school stuff. And the way he kept calling me a "woman" was almost bizarre. How would a *woman* react to what Sam had just said? I had no idea.

Fortunately, Sam didn't seem to expect me to say anything. I shivered as he locked his eyes onto mine and ran his fingertips gently over my arm, making my skin tingle. *I could get used to this,* I thought, gazing back for a long moment. *Yes, I think I could definitely get used to this.*

Finally he pulled his gaze away. "Shall we go?"

I nodded wordlessly, keeping my hand tucked snugly into his arm as we moved down the sidewalk, rounded a corner, and strolled on toward the center of town.

We had walked a couple of blocks, chatting easily about the protest and the first week of school, when Sam paused.

"What is it?" I asked, glancing up at him questioningly. We were still a block or two away from the restaurant.

"Just a second." His mouth was twitching again, as if he was trying to hold back a smile. He gently disengaged my hand from his arm and took two quick steps to the edge of the sidewalk. The block we were on was mostly residential, and there was a large silver mailbox standing in front of the house we were passing. Sam swung open the metal door of the mailbox and reached inside as I watched in puzzlement.

"You don't live here, do you?" I asked. "I thought you lived over by the country club."

"I do. This mailbox belongs to a friend of mine. But I have the strangest feeling that there may be a special delivery for you inside."

I suddenly understood when he pulled out his hand, which was now grasping a bouquet of wildflowers. I gasped as he presented the flowers to me with a flourish.

"*Voilà*," he said, looking pleased at my astonishment. "Beautiful flowers for a beautiful woman. Do you like them?"

"I love them!" I buried my face in the flowers and breathed in their wild, sweet scent. "Thank you. I can't believe you did this for me."

He didn't reply, except by raising my free hand to his lips and brushing my palm with the merest breath of a kiss. I practically fainted—it was just like something out of a romantic old movie.

We continued on our way and soon reached the restaurant. It was early, but Bonne Foi was already bustling. Sam held my arm as we swept past the others to the front of the line. He gave his name, and we were seated within minutes. Sam asked the busboy to bring some water for my flowers along with our drinks.

He thinks of everything, I thought with a warm glow as I watched the busboy scurry away. I turned my gaze to Sam, who was watching me.

"What do you think of the place?" he asked.

I hadn't even had a chance to look around yet, but once I did, I was impressed. The restaurant was casual enough so that my khaki skirt didn't look out of place, but still elegant enough to make me understand why everyone in town was so eager to pay top dollar to go there. "It's great," I said. "Really beautiful."

"I'm glad you like it." Sam reached across the table and took my hand, which was resting on the creamy white tablecloth. "You deserve the best after all you've been through this week, Claudia. I want you to know that there are some of us who appreciate your courage and willingness to stand up for what you believe in."

"Thanks," I said lightly. "I appreciate your appreciation."

Sam smiled briefly, then his face grew serious again. "But that's not the only reason I asked you out," he said softly. "I could never be interested in any woman who didn't have a mind of her own. But I have to admit that the fact that you're the most beautiful girl in school had something to do with my invitation too."

I just about melted at that. Maybe he was laying it on a little thick, but I didn't care. I loved it. How long had it been since anyone had made such an effort to make me feel special? Sam had obviously gone all out in planning this evening down to the last detail. And he wasn't hiding the fact that he saw me as an attractive girl—no, *woman.*

Somehow I can't picture Sam sprawled out on

the sofa in the den, pelting me with cheese curls and burping my name, I thought, remembering a recent afternoon I'd spent with Aaron. I almost laughed at the image, but the sound caught in my throat as I thought about how fast he'd changed into such a jerk. I wondered what he was doing at that moment. Was he thinking about me?

Stop it! I told myself fiercely. *Aaron and I are over.* With some effort, I forced all thoughts of him out of my mind and picked up my menu.

"Everything looks so good," I said brightly, even though I couldn't understand a word on the menu—it was all in French, and I took Spanish.

Sam came to my rescue. "Everything is good here," he said, opening his own menu and glancing over it. "But if you wouldn't mind a recommendation, I think you might like the filet. It's wonderful."

"Mmm, sounds great," I agreed with some relief, not even caring exactly what it might be a filet of. I wasn't a picky eater—as long as it wasn't escargots, I was sure it would be fine. Closing my menu, I sat back in my chair and smiled at Sam as the busboy returned and set out water glasses, then put my flowers into a small vase. "So, where did you hear about those rotten things going on at the university?"

Sam took a sip of his ice water. "I'm glad you asked," he said. "A friend of my cousin's told me about a woman he knew who'd just been fired from the university's English department, and then I started looking into their hiring practices. Do you know that less than five percent of their faculty are minorities?"

I shook my head in disbelief. "That *is* awful," I agreed. "So how did you know what to do about it? I mean, with organizing the rally and everything."

"Oh, I've had a lot of experience with that," Sam replied easily, leaning back in his seat. "I've worked with people in the community before on tons of issues, like the product testing on animals that goes on at that lab on Ridge Road."

My jaw dropped. "How do you find out about all this?" I asked him incredulously.

He shrugged. "It's not that hard to get information when you're looking for it. I get a lot off the Internet, and I talk to other people who care about this stuff as much as I do."

I nodded, barely able to conceal how impressed I was. I'd known Sam had opinions about everything, but it was really interesting the way he researched all these issues and worked hard to change things that he thought were wrong.

"So tell me more about you," Sam said, his eyes shining with interest. "What drove you to get out there and fight for your position on the team?"

I shifted uncomfortably. I hadn't really thought of it that way—I'd just known that I had to play soccer, and being on the guys' team was the only way. I cringed inwardly as I thought about "fighting" for Aaron's position. I had never wanted to take it away from him like that.

"Well, I want to play soccer professionally," I said quickly. "It's kind of my dream to compete in the Olympics someday," I admitted shyly.

"That's wonderful!" Sam exclaimed. "I think it's great to be so ambitious. Don't let anything stand in the way of your goals, Claudia."

I smiled, happy that someone was actually encouraging me instead of telling me I should shove my dreams onto some shelf because the *school* didn't see a need for a girls' soccer team.

Soon our waiter arrived with the filet, which turned out to be fish in a delicate sauce. It was delicious, and I enjoyed it as much as I enjoyed talking to Sam.

My head was spinning from our conversation by the time we left the restaurant. He held the door for me, then put a hand on the small of my back as we stepped out onto the sidewalk. The sky was dark now, with just a few stars twinkling. The air was cooler than it had been earlier, and I shivered slightly as a stray breeze tickled my skin.

Sam looked at me with concern and slid his arm around my waist, pulling me toward him. "Are you cold?"

"Not really." Still, I pressed a little nearer to him as we moved down the sidewalk, heading back toward his car. All that intriguing talk had made me feel very close to Sam, even in the short time we'd been together, and I didn't want the evening to end. He had showed me a new kind of romance, and I was already hooked.

I lifted the flowers up to my face as we walked, inhaling their beautiful scent. "I want to save these to help me remember tonight," I murmured.

Sam's arm tightened around me. "That's nice," he

said. "But I won't need anything to remind me. I'll never forget it."

We walked silently for a moment. I thought about how special this whole evening had been, and how Sam had been the one who'd made it that way. He'd planned every little romantic detail, from the flowers to a delicious dinner, and he'd talked about my soccer dreams as though they were really important. Glancing up at Sam's sharp, handsome profile against the evening sky, I cleared my throat uncertainly. I wasn't ordinarily the least bit shy, but all of a sudden I felt tongue-tied.

"Sam," I said softly.

"Yes?"

I wet my lips. My heart was beating faster, though I wasn't sure why. "Thank you," I whispered.

He stopped walking and turned to face me. We had left the busy downtown area, and only a few other pedestrians were in sight. In the dim yellow light cast by the nearest streetlight, Sam's face looked smooth and shadowy, as if it were sculpted out of marble. He gazed down at me earnestly. "Don't thank me, Claudia," he said, his voice husky. "I'm the one who should thank you."

Before I could answer, he grasped my shoulders and ran his hands down my arms and then around to my back. He bent his head. His lips sought mine, tentative at first, then searching and insistent.

My hands found the back of his neck, burying themselves beneath that thick, lustrous dark honey hair. I let my eyes shut as I sank happily into the kiss.

Eight

Aaron

"OKAY, HAYES," I muttered to myself as I cut the ignition of my mother's car and climbed out. "Here goes nothing."

I wiped my sweaty palms on my shirt as I walked up the brick path toward Hilary's house. Asking her out had been nerve-racking enough, but now that I'd realized I actually had to *take* her out too, I was a total wreck. I'd never really dated much before Claudia, and being with her had been so comfortable and easy that I'd almost forgotten what first dates were like.

Don't sweat it, man, I told myself, thinking back to the pep talk Bruce had given me before leaving for his own date. Bruce wasn't the most eloquent guy in the world, but he was the closest thing to a father figure I had since our dad had died years ago.

And when the subject was girls, at least he spoke from experience. Vast experience. *You already know she likes you, remember?*

I was starting to think that asking Hilary out so soon had been a big mistake. Maybe Claudia could get back to playing the field right away, but the sick feeling in the pit of my stomach seemed to be telling me that I couldn't.

Still, it was too late to back out now. I raised my hand to the doorbell, pausing just long enough for a minor panic attack as I tried to remember if I'd brushed my teeth before I left. After running my tongue over a few molars and tasting mint, I took a deep breath and pressed the bell.

Hilary answered the door herself. She looked fantastic. Her hair was pulled back off her face, she was wearing a white dress that fit her like a second skin, and her lips shimmered with some kind of pink glossy lipstick.

Best of all, she looked thrilled to see me.

"Hi, Aaron," she said in a soft, welcoming voice. "You look great. Would you like to come in?"

"No," I said, but corrected myself quickly. "Uh, I mean, I'd love to. But I thought we'd go see that new action movie downtown, and if we want to eat first . . . um, we should probably get going." I gulped, wondering if I sounded as dorky and stupid as I thought I did. "I mean, if you'd like to see it. It's just a suggestion. I thought we'd grab some burgers at the diner before show time."

She was still smiling. "That sounds nice,"

she agreed. "Just let me get my purse."

Moments later we were on our way. I held the car door for her, trying not to stare as she swung her bare, shapely legs inside.

I hurried back around to the driver's side and climbed in. "Here we go," I said redundantly as I started the engine.

We talked about school as we drove. But we'd pretty much exhausted that thrilling topic by the time we took our seats in one of the deep, wood-paneled booths in the Randallstown Diner. I began to panic as I stared at the girl across the table from me. She was so beautiful, so perfect—and I couldn't think of one intelligent thing to say to her.

I grabbed a menu for cover. Flipping it open, I pretended to examine it carefully, even though Claudia and I had been there so many times that I had it memorized. "Um, I think I'll have the pizza burger," I commented, glancing up to see that Hilary had picked up her menu as well.

"Mmm, that sounds yummy." Hilary set her menu down and smiled at me. "I think I'll have that too."

"Great." Okay, now we'd pretty much covered the whole menu topic as well. What else were we supposed to talk about? "Um, so you're a cheer-leader, huh?"

It wasn't the most brilliant comment anyone had ever made, but Hilary didn't seem to notice. "That's right," she said quickly. "I'm cocaptain of the squad this year." She leaned her elbows on the table and rested her chin on one hand, smiling at me wistfully. "I only wish we had time to cheer at the soccer games as well as the football games. I think the guys who play soccer are so cool."

I gulped. I could practically hear Bruce in my ear: *She's totally into you, man!*

"Thanks," I said smoothly. "I think cheerleaders are pretty cool too."

She giggled and blushed slightly. "Thanks." She paused and then continued shyly, "Do you play a lot of other sports, or just soccer?"

"Oh, yeah," I said eagerly. "Everything except for football, since it's the same season as soccer. Lacrosse is my favorite. Well, no, maybe soccer." I shrugged. "I don't know, I love them both." I grinned. "I guess I'm sort of a sports fanatic," I admitted.

Hilary watched me talk, nodding as if what I was saying were actually important. "Do you have any favorite teams?" she asked.

I flinched, thinking of how many Orioles games Claudia and I had watched together.

"The Redskins," I blurted out, forcing Claudia away from my thoughts. "I mean, I know a lot of people around here like the Ravens, but I'm still a Redskins fan." Ugh, I was even boring *myself.*

I racked my brain for something *not* dull to say, but luckily I was saved from the effort when the waiter came over with our thick, juicy burgers and milk shakes.

"So what other stuff do you like besides sports?" Hilary asked after we'd eaten in silence for a couple of minutes. "Do you like TV? Music? Movies?"

"Sure," I said agreeably. I popped a home-style french fry into my mouth. "Let's see . . . I mainly watch cop shows."

"Me too," Hilary chimed in, her eyes twinkling. "The dramas, right?"

I nodded. "Yeah, like *NYPD Blue*. My favorite kind of music is definitely hard rock—"

"So's mine!" Hilary interrupted.

I sat up straighter in my seat, feeling my confidence level surging.

"And I'm a major movie buff," I added. "*Except* for anything, like, musical. Oh, or cartoons—I really can't deal with those animated movies."

Hilary shook her head. "Me neither," she said, wrinkling her nose in agreement.

I paused to take a sip of my chocolate milk shake. "Actually, though, I have a confession to make."

"What is it?" She leaned forward eagerly, as if afraid of missing a word.

I wiped my mouth with the back of my hand and grinned sheepishly. "My total favorite kind of movies are those old Japanese monster films. You know—Godzilla, Mothra, Gamera, the whole gang."

"Really?" Hilary seemed uncertain whether I was serious or not. "You like those?"

For a moment I felt a little disappointed that she seemed so surprised. *Relax,* I told myself. *You may have a lot in common, but you can't expect her to be your mental identical twin.*

"Really," I told her. "Most people think they're

kind of stupid, but if you approach them with the right frame of mind, they can be really fun. A lot of them are actually metaphors for nuclear war and stuff like that. Plus the effects are cool, and you might be surprised—some of the action scenes are actually pretty scary."

I winced as soon as the words left my mouth. I knew exactly what would have happened if Claudia had been there. *Right, Hayes,* she would say, with that little twist to the corner of her mouth that she got whenever she thought I was being a dork. *A guy in a rubber lizard mask is sooo terrifying. I think I might wet my pants, I'm so scared just thinking about it.*

But Hilary didn't laugh or even smirk. She nodded thoughtfully. "I can see why you'd like them. They're, like, total escapism. Pure fun, you know? Everybody needs that."

Unbelievable. Why had I been so nervous earlier? Being with Hilary was so easy, so totally stress-free. She wasn't interested in teasing me or giving me a hard time. She agreed with practically everything I said, and seemed to understand it all almost before the words came out of my mouth.

Amazing, I thought as I watched her take a delicate bite of her burger. She managed to do it without dripping any grease down her chin at all. *Totally amazing. Who knew dating could be like this?*

I was waiting in the crowded theater lobby for Hilary to emerge from the rest room after the movie when I heard a familiar voice call out my name.

"Yo, Hayes!" Joel said, sauntering up to me. Jason and Rich were right behind him. Joel scratched his chin and looked me up and down. "Check it out, guys," he continued with a smirk. "Hayes is all dressed up in his date-night khakis."

"How about that." Rich smacked me on the shoulder and laughed. "Looks like you owe me ten bucks, Wyman. I told you he'd cave."

"What are you talking about?" Of all the times for them to show up and start acting like dorks . . . I just hoped they'd get lost before Hilary came out. I didn't want her to think all my friends were big losers, or she might decide I was one too.

Jason was the only member of the trio who wasn't grinning like a monkey. In fact, he was giving me a sympathetic look. "It's okay, dude." He shrugged his beefy shoulders. "So you went crawling back to Claudia. It happens."

"Yeah," Joel put in. "She probably threatened to kick his butt if he didn't get back together with her."

"She could do it," Rich agreed.

I scowled at them. They could tell I was on a date, and they just assumed it was with Claudia. Didn't they think I could possibly—

"I'm back, Aaron. Thanks for waiting."

Hilary's honey-sweet voice broke into my thoughts. I hadn't even seen her approaching, but now she linked her arm through mine and gazed into my eyes with a contented smile.

"Whoa," Rich muttered.

Jason was a little less tactful. “Dude,” he said, his tiny blue eyes wide with shock. “You mean you’re here with—with Hilary?”

“Hi, guys,” Hilary said cheerfully. “How’s it going?”

“Not bad,” Joel answered automatically for all of them. As I shot them one last triumphant look and turned to steer Hilary toward the door, I heard him add, “Not bad at all.”

Nine

Claudia

"SURE YOU DON'T want to come?" I asked Jenna as I checked my face in the visor mirror.

"Positive," she replied dryly, steering her car expertly around a pothole on State Street. "Groovy beatnik poetry readings aren't exactly my style. Besides, I don't want to interfere in the romance of the century."

I grinned. "You've got to admit," I said as I pulled out my tinted lip gloss for a quick touch-up, "Sam really knows how to show a girl a good time."

Jenna snorted. "Oh, yeah," she said sarcastically. "Taking you to listen to some lunatic rant and rave about saving the penguins. That's a big step up from hanging out at the diner with Aaron."

"That was a lecture by a really famous professor of zoology," I told her. "Besides, that's not the only interesting thing we've done this week. He also took me to that cool photography exhibit at the college library. And he fixed me that totally romantic picnic before we went to the chamber music concert in the park."

"You told me." Jenna glanced in her rearview mirror as we turned onto a narrow side street. "Cold pasta salad with smoked salmon, wasn't it? I'll give him this much—sounds like he's a better cook than Aaron." She grinned. "Remember when he tried to make you chocolate chip cookies for Valentine's Day and they ended up tasting like garlic because he forgot to wash the bowl?"

I shot her an annoyed glance. "I remember," I said shortly. I also remembered that Aaron had tried to make me give up the sport I loved more than anything. "How could you be all sentimental over the guy after that trick he pulled last Friday anyway?" I asked. "He set me up so the guys could plant that stuff in my locker."

Jenna sighed. "Claud, he could have been talking to Coach Baker about anything. You don't still think he was behind that, do you?" She shook her head. "Aaron wouldn't stoop that low."

I took a deep breath. I had started to doubt it too over the past week. Even when the rest of the team gave me a hard time at practice, Aaron wasn't joining in their pranks. Some part of me really couldn't believe that he would do something that awful to me—but I still didn't know for sure. Forcing a smile, I glanced over at Jenna as she pulled up to the curb in front of the Lyrical Bard Coffeehouse.

"'Fess up," I teased, ignoring her Aaron comment. "The real reason you don't want to come with me is because you're going out with Greg tonight, right?"

"Guilty as charged." Jenna winked.

"Thanks for the ride. Tell the older man I said hi." I flipped the visor back into place, grabbed my sweater from the seat beside me, and opened the car door, waving as Jenna peeled off. I glanced at my watch as I hurried toward the entrance. Sam was meeting me, and I was a little late.

I pushed open the heavy wooden door. I'd never been inside the Lyrical Bard before, and I guess I was expecting something resembling Starbucks. Instead, I found myself stepping into a low-ceilinged, smoky room. A coffee bar was barely visible through the haze at one end of the room, and a small, rickety-looking stage spanned the other side. As I coughed and glanced around for Sam, I felt increasingly out of place. Most of the patrons were older than me—by at least three decades. But more important, the bright red sundress I was wearing made me feel like a clown at a funeral. Just about every person in the room was dressed from head to toe in black.

I had felt pretty good about what I was wearing until that moment. I'd looked forward to seeing Sam's face when he took in the way the thin, silky fabric hugged my body and the short, full skirt swished around my legs when I walked. But now I just wanted to turn around and run out of the place.

I was actually taking a step back toward the door when Sam spotted me and hurried over. "Hi," he said, leaning over to greet me with a quick kiss. "You look fantastic."

"I look like a stoplight," I replied, hugging my white sweater to my chest as if it could possibly hide me. "I didn't realize there was a dress code."

He chuckled. "Don't be silly. It doesn't matter what you wear here."

I raised one eyebrow and looked him up and down. He was wearing black corduroy pants and a black turtleneck. Even the light jacket he had slung over his arm was black.

"Okay, I see your point," he said, following my gaze down to his outfit. "I'm sorry. You look so stunning that I hate to do it, but here." He shook out the folds of his jacket, holding it up so I could slide my arms into the sleeves.

"That's better." I buttoned up the jacket. It covered the colorful dress completely, and I felt more comfortable immediately. I usually didn't mind being different, but I didn't like it to be because of what I was wearing.

Sam reached out and gently touched my cheek. "You can cover up your clothes," he said softly, "but you still stand out in any room you walk into."

I smiled as he put his arms around me and drew me toward him, right there in the entryway of the coffeehouse. As he kissed me hungrily, I couldn't stop thinking about how lucky I was to have found such a wonderful, sensitive, intelligent guy.

Sam pulled back after a long moment, though he kept his arms around me as he gazed into my eyes. "I don't know what I did before I met you," he whispered fervently.

"I don't know either," I replied softly, before pulling his head down to continue our kiss.

The poems all started to sound alike to me after the first few minutes—all the poets had throaty, hoarse voices and talked a lot about birds and dying twilight. Or maybe it was twilight and dying birds. I really wasn't paying much attention. Sam seemed into it, though, so I kept quiet and imagined all the exciting things that lay ahead for us, from the first school dance of the year, which was two weeks away, to the junior prom.

The reading finally ended, and I clapped along with everyone else as the last poet walked off the stage. Sam turned to me. "Wasn't that fantastic?" he commented dreamily. "I mean, wow. The passion!"

I coughed. The smoke had gotten even thicker as the evening progressed. I was starting to understand why all the poets had sounded so hoarse. "Amazing," I croaked. "Um, should we go somewhere and get dessert or something?"

A few minutes later we were seated in a nearby ice cream parlor, sharing a banana split. Sam picked the cherry off the top first thing and fed it to me from his spoon. Aaron had always made me thumb-wrestle for it.

"That was fun," I said, scooping up a spoonful of whipped cream. "I'd never been to a poetry reading before."

"I'm glad you enjoyed it, Claudia." He reached across the small table and clasped my free hand in both of his own. "You know, I really admire the way you're so open to new experiences. That's the sign of a very evolved person."

"Thanks." I was starting to get used to his constant compliments by now.

The little bell on the door tinkled, and I glanced over idly to see who had come in. When I recognized Bruce Hayes and Lisa the Ditz, I frowned.

"What's wrong?" Sam was sitting with his back to the door, so he had to twist his head around to see what I was looking at. "Oh. The Neanderthals are invading."

I giggled nervously, realizing that my body had tensed at the sight of Aaron's brother. Sam was looking at me quizzically, and I shifted in my seat. I hoped Sam wouldn't think that my reaction to Bruce's entrance had something to do with Aaron. I always got uncomfortable around Bruce. Of course, I'd never felt *this* uncomfortable before.

Fortunately, Bruce and Lisa were getting cones to go. They left a couple of minutes later without glancing our way. I turned back to Sam, trying to stay focused in the present. Grasping at the first topic that came into my head, I blurted out, "So guess what? Our first scrimmage is coming up next week. We're playing Meadowfield High on Tuesday."

"Really?" Sam was still staring at me, but the puzzled look was gone, replaced by his usual adoring gaze. "That's great."

I nodded. "Coach Baker has been working us hard this week. I think we'll be ready for them. Our offense—"

"That's the position you play, right?" Sam had loosened his grip on my hand and was stroking my forearm with one finger. It tickled slightly, and I was tempted to pull away. It was hard to eat with just one hand.

"Right. There are three forwards, and I'm one of them." I winced as I thought about having pushed Aaron out of his position. But I hadn't *known* that would happen, I reminded myself. "We're the ones who try to score against the other team," I continued. I licked a spot of chocolate sauce off the handle of my spoon. "Then there are four midfielders, who—"

"I don't care about the other positions." Sam grasped my hand more tightly again, leaning forward. "I only care about you, Claudia."

I smiled. "Sure, but if you're going to come watch my games, you should—"

"I'll only be watching *you,*" he interrupted.

I felt a tiny stab of disappointment. After all the experiences Sam had opened up to me that week, I'd been psyched at the idea of teaching *him* something new.

Still, maybe soccer wasn't the topic for a cultural poetry-reading kind of evening. Besides, thinking about soccer made me think about Aaron, and I didn't want to do that. Not that night. Not at all. I was trying to forget Aaron and I had ever been anything more than teammates.

I looked at Sam, sheer force of will replacing the image of Aaron in my mind with Sam's handsome, angular face. The soccer lesson could wait for a more appropriate time, such as the football game the next day. We'd talked about getting together on Saturday but hadn't made any plans yet, and I was hoping Sam would want to go to the game with me.

"By the way," I said, dropping my spoon in the dish.

Before I could go on, Sam leaned even farther forward, clasping both my hands in his. "Claudia, you're so incredible," he said smoothly. "I've actually composed a poem for you. Would you like to hear it?"

I nodded wordlessly. Once again Sam had managed to completely amaze me. A poem for me—what could be more romantic than that? He cleared his throat and closed his eyes, as if composing his thoughts. I sat still, hardly daring to breathe.

"Beautiful redbird," he intoned, his eyes still closed, his voice low and dramatic. "Flying into my life with the force of a thousand imploding suns, / How free you are, and how lovely, / Like the first star that appears against the dying light of the evening sun. / I want to join your flight, and sing your praises to the moon. / Beautiful bird, stay with me."

"Wow," I breathed as he opened his eyes and gazed at me expectantly. The poem hadn't made much sense to me, but what did I know about poetry?

The point was, he had composed it for *me*. "I mean—wow. I don't know what to say."

He looked pleased. "Say you'll spend the afternoon with me tomorrow."

"Actually, I was going to suggest the same—"

"Good." Sam put one hand to my face, stroking my cheek with his thumb. "Because I've got a special day planned. There's a lecture on making your voice heard in today's society, and then I figured we could go to Bonne Foi for dinner again."

I felt a pang as I realized the football game was out of the question. But it passed quickly. The season was young—there would be other football games.

"That sounds great," I replied, trying to muster some enthusiasm.

"And there's something else I want to ask you," Sam said, his voice deepening. My eyes widened at his serious tone.

"What?" I asked him, sitting up straighter in anticipation.

"Claudia," he began huskily, taking my hands in his again and staring into my eyes intently, "I'm happier than I ever thought possible because we're together. Will you make my happiness complete by being my date for the fall dance?"

I shivered. "Yes," I whispered, my heart racing. "I would love to."

I watched his face light up at my answer, and I wondered in awe how I'd ended up with the most romantic guy on the planet.

Ten

Aaron

"RANDALLSTOWN RULES!" JASON crowed, raising both hands toward me. "We rule!"

I slapped his hands. "Yeah," I agreed. "What an awesome game."

The other guys we'd been sitting with jostled and clambered around on the bleachers, talking excitedly about the football team's close win over County High. But the game we'd just watched was already fading from my mind as I watched Hilary prance off the field with the other cheerleaders. I was supposed to meet her after she showered and changed so that we could go out.

Rich noticed where my gaze was focused and grinned knowingly. "And I thought you came today to support your brother," he joked. "But all the time you were just enjoying the scenery."

Jason turned to watch the cheerleaders too. "Hey, I don't blame you, man. If I were going out with Hilary, I'd never take my eyes off her either."

"You never take your eyes off her as it is," Joel spoke up. "You'd better watch it, Kent, or Hayes might have to kick your butt."

Rich smirked and gave me a sidelong glance. "Or maybe he'll get his ex to do it for him."

I shot him a dirty look. Breaking up with Claudia had saved me from the worst of their teasing, but that didn't mean they were letting me off easy. They still ragged me about her every chance they got. "I'm out of here," I muttered. "I've got better things to do than sit around and listen to you morons all day."

They laughed and made kissing noises at my back as I stepped across the empty bleacher in front of me and headed for the metal stairs. I was annoyed that they'd brought up Claudia—now I couldn't stop myself from scanning the crowds, looking for her familiar brown ponytail. I hadn't seen her yet, but I was sure she was there. She never missed a home game if she could help it. I wondered if her dad had come with her, or if she'd dragged that pathetic jerk Wrightfield along. . . .

Stop it! I ordered myself sternly. *Forget her. You're with Hilary now, remember? That should be enough to make you forget just about anything.*

Thinking about the past week with Hilary did make me feel better. I took the steps two at a time as I did a mental review of our dates. We'd caught another movie on Sunday, and on Wednesday I'd taken her bowling. It was kind of a relief to go out with a girl who couldn't even come close to beating my score. She'd looked at me as if I were the greatest bowler in the history of the world, even though I'd thrown only one strike the whole afternoon. She had a way of doing that—of making me feel as though everything I did was perfect, even when it wasn't. The night before, we'd even shared my ultimate fantasy date—takeout Chinese food in front of a Godzilla marathon on cable. During the commercials, her kisses had tasted like sweet-and-sour sauce. Heaven.

I was leaning on the wall outside the girls' locker room when she emerged fifteen minutes later, looking fresh-scrubbed and glowing in a short dress. I think the dress was blue, like her eyes, but I didn't really take in the details because I was too busy admiring her long, smooth legs.

She greeted me with a kiss. "Pretty good game, huh?" she commented brightly. "Your brother was great."

"Awesome," I agreed, reaching into my pocket for the keys to my truck. "Ready to go?"

"Sure. Um, did you make any plans yet? Because I thought maybe we could go over to Anna Yan's place for a while. She and some of the other cheerleaders and their boyfriends are getting together to pick out CDs to play at the school dance." She glanced at me shyly from under slightly lowered lashes. "We promised Principal Carter we'd take care of the music."

She seemed pretty excited about the whole idea, so I didn't have the heart to say no, even though it didn't sound like much fun to me. Hilary was great, but Anna Yan and her other friends on the cheerleading squad spent most of their time talking about shopping and eye shadow and boring stuff like that. Hanging out with them wouldn't be quite the romantic Saturday afternoon I'd had in mind.

"Okay," I said, trying to muster up some fake enthusiasm. After all, how long could the little CD party last? Hilary and I would still have all evening to be together. "Sounds like a plan."

She peered up into my face, looking worried. "Are you sure?" she asked tentatively. "I mean, it's just an idea. We don't have to do it if you don't want to. Did you have something else you wanted to do?"

Well, since she'd asked . . . "Nothing major." I shrugged and put my arms on her shoulders, my fingers playing with her reddish hair. I moved a little closer until my lips were at her forehead. "I was just thinking we'd grab some food and hang out at my place. Alone. You know."

She tilted her face up toward mine, standing on tiptoe to kiss me softly on the tip of my nose. "You know what?" she whispered. "Let's do that instead. They don't really need us at Anna's."

"Are you sure?"

She nodded quickly. "It's no big deal. I'd rather be with you."

Her words were music to my ears. It was so great to be with someone whose first priority was me.

I kissed her, and I didn't pull away until some of her friends emerged from the locker room and started giggling. Then I decided we'd better get going before we got dragged along to Anna's CD party after all.

Thinking about those CDs reminded me that I hadn't asked Hilary to the dance yet. Actually, I'd sort of blocked out all thoughts of the dance. It had been at a school dance just before Christmas vacation the year before when Claudia and I had first gotten together. It had taken me most of the evening to work up the guts to ask her to dance, and when she'd said yes, I'd been so surprised that I just stood there like a dork for about thirty seconds.

I knew it was stupid to still be so hung up on memories such as that. It was time to make some new memories, starting now. "So, Hil," I said, keeping my arm around her shoulders as I led her toward the parking lot. "Speaking of that dance, I've been meaning to ask you. Wanna go with me?"

She glanced up at me quickly. "Sure," she said immediately. "I'd love to."

Good. That was settled. I briefly wondered if Claudia would be at the dance with her dorky new man. But I chased the thought away just as quickly as it had come. It didn't matter. What Claudia did didn't matter to me at all anymore.

Eleven

Claudia

"YOU'RE LATE, WILLOUGHBY," Coach Baker barked. "Get warmed up. We've got a lot to do today."

"Okay, Coach," I said, hurrying onto the field. "Sorry."

It wasn't like me not to be on time for soccer practice, but Sam had been waiting for me after my last class, all excited because he'd just heard about a poetry reading in town that evening and wanted to know if I could go with him.

It was over a week after our first date. But our relationship had had a whirlwind first six days, and I was loving every minute. Sam and I were living life to the fullest, doing interesting things every time we got together.

Our plans are proof enough of that, I thought

giddily as I joined my other teammates, who were already warming up for practice. *Me, Claudia Willoughby, going to another poetry reading. What are the odds?* I had to smile at the thought.

My gaze wandered across the field as I did a few stretches on the sidelines. I couldn't help seeking out Aaron first. At the moment his back was to me as he passed a ball back and forth with Charlie Donnelly. No matter how happy I was with Sam, I couldn't help feeling a pang as I took in the familiar sight of my ex-boyfriend playing the sport we both loved. How could we have become strangers so fast?

I grabbed a spare ball and jogged onto the field, dribbling slowly. The guys were ignoring me at the moment, which was a relief. Most of them had been hassling me all week every chance they got—which meant anytime the coach wasn't looking.

Just then Charlie sent a wild kick right past Aaron. "Heads up!" he shouted.

I had already seen the ball hurtling my way. Quickly pushing my own ball aside, I took a couple of steps forward to head off the runaway, lifting one knee and bouncing it off to the side. I reached out and caught it in the air.

"Thanks, Claudia," Charlie called. "Sorry about that."

"It's okay," I said, actually meaning it for a change. Charlie was a nice guy—ever since that first practice, he'd been treating me like a teammate, unlike the other starters.

I noticed Aaron turn to look at me. His gaze was neutral, and he didn't say a word. I stared back at him for a moment, realizing that actual eye contact was a major breakthrough for us at this point.

I cleared my throat. "Here," I said, tossing the ball to Aaron, who was closer than Charlie.

He bounced the ball off the inside of his calf, bringing it smoothly into line between his feet. "Thanks," he replied.

Then he spun away and shot the ball back to Charlie. I turned away too, wondering why that one little word—the first he'd spoken directly to me in more than a week, since the last day of tryouts—made me feel so weird and sad and confused all at once.

I was still feeling kind of rattled when Coach Baker called us to attention a few minutes later. I turned to kick my practice ball back toward the sidelines, then did my best to concentrate as the coach started talking, setting us up for a passing drill.

Jason was in the goal, and the rest of us split up into two lines on either side. The first person on one side would take the ball, dribble for a few yards, then pass to the first person on the other side, who would take a shot. Then they both went to the back of the line so that the next pair could come forward and take their turn.

Coach Baker had intentionally made the two

lines uneven so that different players would be paired up each time. He watched us carefully for the first few rounds, probably making sure no one pulled anything stupid with me. Rich Tarvell passed me the ball cleanly, but he kicked it a little harder than necessary. It wasn't anything I couldn't handle, though, and I shot the ball straight into Jason's waiting hands.

On the second round it was my turn to pass to Charlie. My shot was clean, and Charlie received it easily and made the goal.

After a few more pairs had taken their turns, the coach told us to keep going. Then he wandered off to check on the JV players, who were scrimmaging on the next field.

I started feeling a little nervous when I noticed the guys in the opposite line talking to one another and shooting me glances. I could only imagine what they were planning for me when my next turn came. Maybe they'd wing the ball straight at my face in the hopes of knocking out a few of my teeth. Or maybe they'd just overshoot so that I'd have to go pounding off after the ball and look like an idiot if the coach happened to glance over.

Counting down the line, I bit my lip. I was lined up against Joel Wyman. He'd been one of my most relentless tormenters all along, and I knew he was capable of almost anything. Still, I wasn't about to let him see that I was afraid.

When my turn came, I stepped forward. But

instead of coming to intercept the ball as Jason tossed it out, Joel suddenly turned and shoved Aaron, who was behind him, onto the field. Aaron looked startled as most of the other guys on both sides started laughing.

I felt my face flame up as I realized what was happening. Joel wanted Aaron to be the one to humiliate me. My fists clenched automatically at my sides. I waited for the pass, expecting the worst.

But it didn't come. After his initial surprise, Aaron managed to recover and grab the ball. He shot Joel a dirty look, then dribbled in place for a moment, making sure he had full control before starting forward.

He glanced over at me briefly and I saw that his expression was totally focused, the way it always got when he was deep into a play. All of my tension melted away, and my body sort of took over. It was as if we had both flashed back in time and were in my backyard again, practicing drills together the way we'd done all summer long.

I moved forward smoothly, keeping my eye on Aaron and the ball. At just the right moment he made the pass, fast and accurate. I stopped it expertly, continuing the momentum as I turned and shot, sending the ball whizzing straight past Jason and into the net.

With a smile of triumph, I glanced over to see what Aaron thought of my shot. He was grinning back at me, and I felt a burst of happiness. Then he quickly looked away, jogging back to the end of his line.

My heart sank. Had I just been imagining things? Was it totally crazy to think Aaron and I had been connecting out there? I didn't know *what* to think.

The rest of practice was uneventful, but I was completely distracted. When we finished, I found myself walking back toward the locker rooms a few strides behind Aaron. He was alone, looking worn-out after the tough workout. I quickened my pace to catch up with him, curious about that moment on the field.

"Hey," I greeted him when I reached his side. "Good practice, huh?"

He blinked at me, looking startled. But he recovered quickly. "Yeah."

It wasn't exactly an encouraging response, but at least he was being civil. I took it as a sign to keep trying.

"So, about that locker trick," I said, watching his face carefully.

He stared back at me, his brow furrowing in confusion. My heart leaped at the way he seemed genuinely puzzled. Jenna was right—Aaron *hadn't* been behind that.

"Huh?" he asked.

At that moment there was a shrill squeal from the direction of the school building. It sounded like a pig being slaughtered. But when I looked in the direction of the noise, I realized it was just Hilary Walters calling Aaron's name. She was hurrying toward us, waving at Aaron and looking as perky and empty-headed as always. I'd seen them around school together, and I'd heard rumors. But somehow it had been hard for me to believe that Aaron could ever fall for someone like her. I felt a pang as I saw Aaron's face light up when he saw her. *It's true,* I realized with a sinking heart.

"Bimbo alert," I muttered to myself.

Or at least I thought it was to myself. But I guess my voice came out a little louder than I'd meant it to, because Aaron shot me an irritated glance.

"What's the matter, Claudia?" he snapped. "Jealous?"

All of my wishes for peace with Aaron flew out the window. He should have known better than anyone that there was no way I could ever be jealous of a loser airhead like Hilary. "As *if,*" I shot back, my voice wavering slightly. "I hope you're having fun with her, Aaron. But don't forget to put her back in the box when you're finished."

He didn't bother to answer. He just shot me a quick, disgruntled glare and then hurried forward to meet Hilary.

I turned my face away as I walked past them. I couldn't watch them together. Especially not just then. I was already feeling sick to my stomach.

* * *

"I don't think you understand," Greg said in a calm, reasonable tone. "All I'm saying is that there are two sides to every story. And I think the university administration had some valid reasons for letting Professor Abrams go."

Sam had a stubborn look on his face that I hadn't seen before. "Sure they did. If the fact that she's African-American is a valid reason."

Jenna rolled her eyes at me when the guys weren't looking. Their argument had been going on for a good ten minutes now. I ignored her, staring at the pizza burger on the plate in front of me. I couldn't understand it. It was Friday night, I was with my new boyfriend and my best friend at my favorite diner, and I was feeling grumpier by the moment.

The two guys didn't notice my annoyance, but Jenna did. "Are you okay, Claudia?" she asked.

I kept my eyes on my food and murmured something vague. For some reason, Sam's impassioned speech about racial discrimination was rubbing me the wrong way that night. I knew it was a topic he cared a lot about, but did that mean he couldn't let Greg get a word in edgewise? After all, Greg went to the university—he knew the professor who'd been fired. Surely he had something useful to say. Couldn't Sam just stop and listen?

Jenna didn't look satisfied by my response. "I've got to hit the ladies' room," she said casually. "Keep me company, Claud?"

Inside the tiny rest room near the diner's noisy kitchen, Jenna went straight to the white sink and starting examining her eyeliner in the cracked mirror. "Okay, now admit it," she said. "After the third time Sam used the phrase 'discriminatory hiring practices,' weren't you ready to throttle him?"

I had been, but I wasn't about to admit it, even to Jenna. "I don't know what you mean," I said haughtily. "I thought Sam was making some very good points."

Jenna glanced at my reflection in the mirror, looking surprised. "No way. You mean you haven't come to your senses yet, even after that pompous monologue?" She let out a short laugh of disbelief. "Come on. I know you're on the rebound from Aaron, but still . . ."

"I am not," I said quickly, folding my arms across my chest. "This has nothing to do with Aaron. I mean, maybe part of the reason I first went out with Sam was to help me get over the breakup. But he's a wonderful, caring person. He never lets me forget how crazy he is about me."

"Sam's a dork," Jenna replied bluntly. "You can do better. You *have* done better."

"Give me a break," I said, feeling defensive. "Sam might not be perfect. But what guy is? Aaron certainly didn't come close."

Jenna stared at me. "Maybe Aaron isn't perfect either. But at least you had something in common with him."

"Sam and I love being together," I snapped. "That's all we need to have in common."

Jenna pursed her cherry-colored lips and gave me a skeptical look. "Right," she said. "From where I sit, it looks like the only thing you two have in common is you both think he's the greatest thing since sliced bread."

"Just drop it, okay?" I brushed past her and stomped out of the bathroom. I returned to the table and forced myself to sit there for another ten minutes before giving up on the evening. Pretending I had a headache, I asked Sam to take me home early.

When I woke up the next morning, I was sure it all had been just a passing grumpy mood. My irritation with Sam felt like a fading dream as I got dressed and went downstairs. Dad had gotten up early to make his special blueberry-pecan pancakes for breakfast, and he and Mom and I sat around the table for almost an hour, stuffing ourselves and catching up after our busy week.

After breakfast Sam arrived to pick me up, greeting me with his usual lingering kiss, and we drove into town, planning to browse in the bookstore for a while and then grab some lunch. He spent most of the drive talking about global warming, but I wasn't really listening. Some of my disgruntled feelings from the night before had crept back as soon as I'd seen him, and I wasn't sure why.

As we pulled into the small parking lot behind the bookstore, Sam changed the subject, mentioning an art exhibit that was coming to a museum in D.C. the following week.

"It's supposed to be the most complete gathering of the artist's work in decades," he told me enthusiastically. "I pulled some strings, and I got us tickets for the opening day of the exhibit next Saturday—the day after the big dance. What do you say?"

"I can't do it then," I said, a little surprised that he even had to ask. "I have our first official game that day, remember? We're playing Westville."

"Oh, right." Sam frowned as he pulled the car neatly into a vacant parking spot and cut the engine. It was clear that he'd forgotten all about the game, even though he'd assured me just a few days earlier that he was dying to come watch me play.

"It's okay," I said, wondering with apprehension if Jenna had been on to something after all. Sam cared about stuff like art exhibits. I cared about soccer. Were we just too different from each other? "I'm sure you can find someone else to go with you."

"Don't be ridiculous." He turned to smile at me as he unsnapped his seat belt. "I just got the dates mixed up. I wouldn't miss your big game for the world. We can see the exhibit another time."

My doubts quickly faded. *So there, Jenna!* I thought smugly. *Whatever his other interests might be, Sam's main interest is me, and that's all that matters.*

I was smiling as we walked hand in hand into the bookstore, which was already crowded with weekend shoppers. There were several large tables scattered across the open expanse of floor near the register, all of them stacked high with new releases, and I immediately spotted a familiar cover among the jumble of bright dust jackets.

I gasped and rushed forward. "Look!" I exclaimed, grabbing a picture book called *Petie the Pet Store Parrot.* "This was my favorite book when I was a kid. They must have just rereleased it or something."

"Really? Let's see it." Sam picked up another copy of the book and flipped through it quickly. After a moment he dropped it back on the table with a look of disgust. "That?" he said disdainfully. "You've got to be kidding. The publisher should be boycotted."

My eyes widened, and I clutched the copy I was holding to my chest. "What are you talking about?" I demanded. "It's a sweet story."

"It's a tacit sanctioning of the puppy-mill industry that supplies pet stores with poorly treated animals." Sam shook his head and gave me a pitying look. "I know you were just a child, but surely you can see the problem now, can't you? By supporting those who produced this book, we have to accept responsibility for supporting the suffering of helpless creatures."

I frowned, my happy mood vanishing as quickly as it had come. "It's just a kids' book," I muttered.

Sam didn't hear me. He'd wandered to a different table and found the latest book by his favorite experimental poet, a thin hardcover titled *Loss, Yearning, and My Soul.* He leaped toward it, already exclaiming about the depth of the poet's imagery and the courage of his verse. Or something.

All I could think about was a movie I'd seen with Aaron once. It had been awful—I didn't even remember what it was called. But there was this scene in which the hero, a pumped-up action star with more muscles than talent, had somberly told the heroine that he *yearned* for her. For some reason, the way he'd said it had totally cracked us up. For weeks afterward we'd regularly greeted each other by saying, "Hi. How's it going? I yearn for you."

I squashed the memory as fast as I could. "I'll be right over here, okay?" I told Sam, moving toward a nearby table. I picked up the first book I came to, which happened to be a paperback romance novel called *Forgive and Forget.* I decided to take it as a hint from the universe. I had to forgive Sam for not being quite as perfect as I'd thought he was at first. After all, he was a human being like the rest of us. And more important, I had to forget about Aaron once and for all.

Tossing the novel back on the table, I pasted a smile on my face and headed back to where Sam was paging through his poetry book. He glanced up as I reached him, his blue eyes gleaming. "Listen to this," he said eagerly. "It's a poem called 'Death of a Chickadee.'"

He went on to read the poem aloud in a dramatic and rather loud voice, causing several other customers and a salesclerk to turn and stare. My new resolution crumbled as I seriously considered smacking Sam upside the head to stop his ridiculous public reading. Didn't he even realize how silly he looked to other people sometimes? Didn't he even care that half the school thought he was a joke, and the other half thought he was a snob?

I caught myself at that thought. What was wrong with me? Since when did I care what other people thought?

That's not really the point, I admitted to myself. *It's not what other people think of Sam that's bothering me. It's what* I'm *starting to think of him.*

Sam finally finished his impromptu reading and set the poetry book back on the table. "Oh, please," he commented, poking at a pile of thick hardcovers nearby. "Look at this, Claudia. Can you believe they put a masterpiece like *Loss, Yearning, and My Soul* on the same table with this illiterate drivel?"

I looked at the drivel in question and gulped. So much for not thinking about Aaron anymore. The book Sam was indicating was a large, glossy coffee-table volume about Japanese monster movies, Aaron's favorite genre of all time.

"Bummer," I said blandly. All of a sudden I just wanted to get out of the bookstore. It seemed to be bringing out the worst in Sam—and in me. "Listen," I said, putting a hand on his arm. "What do you say we ditch this place? We could go back to my house, maybe make some popcorn, and watch the Penn State game with my dad."

Sam stared at me in astonishment. "Football?" he asked. "You actually want to sit and watch a bunch of stupid blockheads ram into each other? Talk about a waste of time."

I took a deep breath, totally fed up with his attitude. Didn't he realize that by insulting stuff like college football—not to mention *Petie the Pet Store Parrot*—he was also insulting me? Before I could get control of my anger enough to speak, his gaze fell on another book on the table in front of us. "Oh, I've been waiting for this to come out. I'll be right back—I'm going to go ask the manager if the author's doing a book signing here." He rushed off toward the back of the store.

I was relieved to see him go. Collapsing against the edge of the nearest table, I tried to sort out my jumbled thoughts. My indignation about his sports comment had already faded as I realized that he hadn't meant it personally. After all, Sam had strong opinions about everything. I'd known that from the beginning—it was one of the things I'd found so attractive about him. Maybe he went overboard sometimes. But I couldn't expect him to censor his thoughts just to protect me. I wouldn't want him to.

I just wish more of his opinions were the same as mine. The thought startled me. Maybe what Jenna had said the night before had stuck with me more than I'd realized.

It wasn't that I didn't support most of the causes Sam believed in. Equal rights, fair hiring practices, kindness to animals—it was all cool with me. I just didn't know if I was ready to be with someone who was so passionate about issues that he couldn't take any time off from them. I was glad I'd had a chance to experience new things, such as the lectures and the protest rally and even the poetry readings. But I missed just kicking back and hanging out sometimes, acting goofy and watching TV.

I sighed, looking down at my watch. Since when was I this anxious for a date to be over?

I heard a jangle of bells and glanced over at the store's front door.

"Aaron," I whispered.

He looked so familiar that a sense of déjà vu washed over me, making my knees almost shake. Had these last few weeks been a bad dream? Maybe I had imagined our breakup, and now I was back to real life, waiting to meet Aaron here so we could browse through the new magazines before heading over to my house to watch the Penn State game on TV. . . .

I shook off those crazy thoughts as quickly as

they'd come. *This is real life, all right,* I reminded myself. *But Aaron and I are over.*

Just then Aaron spotted me. He looked startled and panicky for a second, sort of the way he always looked when he realized there were three or four defenders between him and the goal and not much time left on the clock.

"Hello, Claudia," he said at last, his voice formal but not unfriendly.

Hi. How's it going? I yearn for you. The words formed in my mind before I could stop them. I cleared my throat. "Hey, Aaron."

I'd almost forgotten what it was like to look straight at him and have him return the look without scowling. I ran my eyes over his familiar face, the slouchy jeans I'd helped him pick out at the mall a few months earlier, and his favorite Orioles T-shirt. How could he look so much the same when things were so different now?

Aaron glanced at his watch. "What are you doing here?" he asked. "The Penn State game starts in twenty minutes."

A feeling of warmth swept through me at his words, so quick and unexpected that it took my breath away. I didn't know why I should be so surprised—it had been only a couple of weeks since we'd broken up. But right then it seemed like a small miracle that Aaron remembered my habits so well after everything that had happened.

I tried to shove that aside, to summon up my anger at him. But instead, all I could seem to think about was the good stuff. Nine months of being together, knowing each other better than anyone else, loving each other . . . It was too sad to think that all that was over.

Maybe I was too quick to let it end, I thought. *Maybe we could have worked things out somehow.*

Part of me couldn't believe I was thinking that after the things he'd said and done. But another part didn't care—I just wanted everything back the way it had been. Sam was interesting and new, but Aaron and I fit together so well. We knew all of each other's quirks inside and out.

"Hey, check it out," I said, stepping aside and gesturing at the monster-movie book on the table behind me. "Have you seen this?"

Aaron's eyes lit up when he spotted the book. "Not yet," he said, stepping forward and grabbing a copy. "It's what I came in here for." He flipped through the book eagerly.

I moved closer to glance over his shoulder, watching photo after photo of ridiculously fake giant lizards and insects and other monsters go by. "Wow," I commented. "It's scary how many of those stupid creatures I actually recognize thanks to you."

"Hey, what can I say? I'm a good influence." Aaron glanced up at me and grinned.

Our eyes met, and his grin faded. We stared at each other for what seemed like an eternity, though it was probably only about three seconds. I felt frozen in place, unable to move or even blink. The busy, noisy store surrounding us faded away, and all I could see was Aaron standing close in front of me, his searching eyes seeming to stare straight into my soul. For the first time I recognized how much I really missed him, how I ached to reach for him and kiss him until all our problems went away. . . .

"Anyway," Aaron said, his voice husky, "I, uh, I'd better get going or I'll miss kickoff." His eyes didn't leave my face. "Want to walk me out?"

There was nothing I wanted more. The way he was looking at me, the expression in his dark eyes . . . Could he be thinking and feeling some of the same things that I was? Maybe there really was still a chance for us.

Wait. I can't leave the bookstore. I'm here with Sam. I felt a wave of disappointment and tried to think of an excuse I could give Aaron. Somehow I just didn't want to mention Sam's name to him—not right then. But even if Sam didn't turn up and blow my cover, Aaron would spot it right away if I tried to lie. He always did.

"Um, I can't. I'm not—I mean, Sam is—Sam and I are here together," I finally admitted, forcing the words out in what I hoped was a casual and matter-of-fact tone. "He's around here somewhere."

I was sure I saw a shadow of emotion cross Aaron's face. But his next words shattered my illusions. "That's great," he said. "I'm glad you and Sam are as happy together as Hilary and I are." He shrugged and held up the book he was holding. "Actually, Hil was the one who told me about this book. She heard about it and knew I'd love it."

Hil?

"Oh. That's nice." I kept my voice neutral, but inside I felt my stomach churning and my heart twisting into knots. I couldn't believe I'd just been thinking that Aaron and I could get back together. What was wrong with me? Aaron was obviously content with his new girlfriend—his pretty, vacant, no-mind-of-her-own, total-opposite-of-me girlfriend. I couldn't let him see how much it bothered me to realize that.

At that moment I spotted Sam coming toward me, his nose buried in another book. Hurrying over, I greeted him with a long, intense kiss. Sam was clearly taken by surprise, but he didn't let that stop him for long. He wrapped his arms around me and kissed me back with enthusiasm.

That should show Aaron, I thought with satisfaction as I kissed Sam. *That should prove that he's not the only one who's moved on.*

When I came up for air and glanced over my shoulder to see his reaction, however, I was disappointed. Aaron hardly seemed to have noticed my show of affection for Sam. He was strolling toward the register, holding his monster book.

Meanwhile, Sam was gazing down at me with a big smile on his face. "Well," he joked, "I'm glad to see you missed me so much. I'll have to leave you alone more often."

I forced myself to return his smile, glad that he apparently hadn't noticed Aaron's presence at all. "Don't you dare," I joked back.

He hugged me to him. "Don't worry," he murmured into my hair. "I'd be a fool to let a beautiful woman like you out of my sight too often."

I closed my eyes and relaxed against his chest. Maybe Sam wasn't perfect. But at least he appreciated me, and he made no secret of it. I would just have to remember that his outspoken opinions were a part of him, a part I would learn to accept.

I should be glad Sam has his own opinions, his own personality, I told myself as Sam stroked the back of my neck and kissed me on the temple. *Not like Little Miss Clueless, Hilary Walters.*

Twelve

Aaron

I TRIED NOT to let it bother me. But seeing Claudia kiss that phony, self-righteous jerk in front of the whole world, or at least the whole bookstore . . .

I was still seething about it hours later as Hilary and I hiked along one of my favorite trails in the state park. She had rushed home from cheering at the football team's away game to be with me, which should have made me feel better about things. But for some reason, her eagerness to make me happy was kind of getting on my nerves.

"Are you sure you want to go all the way to the waterfall?" I asked her for about the third time since we'd started hiking fifteen minutes earlier. "It's at least three or four miles round-trip."

"I'm sure," she panted, clambering over a large

log that had fallen over the trail. "You said it's the coolest trail, right? I want to see it with you."

I stood back, momentarily distracted by the view of her from behind as she crested the log. But as I hopped easily over the obstacle, I slipped back into the state of mild irritation that had come over me when she'd cheerfully admitted as we started out that she'd never been hiking before. "You'll just have to teach me everything you know," she'd told me. I didn't know why that bothered me so much.

There was only one way to cheer myself up, I decided. "Hey, Hilary," I said. "Stop for a minute. There's one very important rule of hiking I forgot to tell you about."

She stopped obediently, turning to look at me. "What is it?"

I took a step closer. "The frequent-kissing rule." I shrugged and grinned. "It's sort of a safety thing, you know. Helps you make sure your hiking partner doesn't get lost or anything."

She giggled and snaked her arms up my chest to my shoulders. "Oh, really?" she said mischievously. "Well, I'm not very good at learning new rules. So we'd better practice that one a lot."

We kissed for a few minutes, but it didn't have the effect it usually did. My mind kept wandering. Mostly it wandered straight back to the bookstore and the way that doofus Wrightfield had run his hands over Claudia's hair. . . .

I broke away first. Hilary smiled up at me. "Mmm, that was nice," she murmured.

"Yeah," I agreed halfheartedly, feeling guilty for thinking about another girl while I was kissing her. Especially a girl I shouldn't be thinking about at all. "Well, we should probably keep moving. Like I said, it's quite a way to the waterfall."

"Okay." Hilary reached into her jeans pocket as we started down the trail again, pulling out a tiny compact and a lipstick. I pretended not to watch as she touched up her makeup, though I cringed and almost grabbed her when she came within millimeters of tripping over an exposed root in the trail.

I relaxed a little when she put the makeup away. For a while we hiked along without incident. We were moving a little more slowly than I would have preferred, but it was a beautiful fall day and I was enjoying being out in the woods, breathing in fresh air and listening to lively birdsongs all around me. Hilary, Claudia, soccer, and everything else faded as I moved down the trail one step at a time.

"Ouch!" Hilary's exclamation broke into my Zen state. She collapsed onto the ground, grabbing at her left hiking boot. "Oh, ow ow ow! Aaron, help me!"

"What's wrong?" I asked, alarmed. I hadn't been paying much attention, and I was afraid she'd twisted her ankle or something.

But it turned out she'd just gotten a tiny stone in her boot. I helped her pull the boot off, dumping the offending pebble into the leaf mold at the side of the trail. Then I handed the boot back to her.

"Thank you so much, Aaron," she cooed, leaning

forward to give me a peck on the cheek. "That's much better."

I watched as she fussed with her laces. "Nice boots," I commented, wondering why she would buy top-of-the-line hiking boots if she didn't hike. "Have you had them long?"

She glanced up at me and laughed. "Of course not, silly," she said. "I just bought them yesterday." She stretched her hand upward, waiting for me to help her up.

I pulled her to her feet, and we continued on our way. "You mean you bought them just for today?" I'd suspected as much as soon as I'd seen the shiny leather and stiff laces, but for some reason, I wanted to hear her admit it.

"Sure. Why not?" She seemed a little surprised at the question.

Why not is right, I told myself. *What's the big deal? They're only a pair of boots.*

But it bothered me that she had rushed out to buy expensive new hiking boots simply because I'd suggested a trek in the park. Why hadn't she just told me she didn't have the right shoes? We could have done something else—maybe something *she* wanted to do for a change.

I felt like a traitor to my entire gender. Wasn't I living every guy's fantasy? I was dating a gorgeous girl who was crazy about me, who was thrilled to do whatever I suggested, from hiking to watching ESPN to spending the evening at the bowling alley. Anything I did, she thought was wonderful.

Anything I said, she thought was brilliant. Anywhere I wanted to go, she wanted to go too. It should have been the perfect situation. So what was my problem?

I missed having someone to argue with—someone who challenged me and didn't let me get away with being a jerk.

I missed Claudia.

I remembered the last time Claudia and I had gone hiking. It had been a hot, incredibly humid day in August, so sticky and oppressive that even the shade of the woods hadn't provided much relief. We'd taken this very trail, and we'd hardly gone half a mile when Claudia had challenged me to race her to the waterfall. I'd accepted, of course, and we'd taken off, swimming through the heavy air and laughing all the way. She'd tried to trip me a few times, I'd elbowed my way past her a few times, and in the end, we'd reached the grassy clearing beside the waterfall at the same time. We'd both been practically on the verge of heatstroke and too exhausted to speak, but with one glance we'd reached an agreement. I'd taken her hand, we'd both kicked off our shoes, and then we'd raced for the cool, clear water, splashing into the stream together and ducking beneath the waterfall.

I sighed, remembering how cute she'd looked that day, with her hair plastered to her head and her cheeks bright red from exertion, laughing and trying to dunk me. I also remembered how great she'd looked a few hours earlier at the bookstore. . . .

"Penny for your thoughts." Hilary interrupted my

momentary lapse into nostalgia, squeezing my elbow gently and tilting back her head to look into my face.

I glanced at her, feeling guilty for thinking about Claudia during our date. It wasn't Hilary's fault I couldn't seem to figure out how to feel about anything these days. "No deal," I joked. "My mind's a total blank, as usual. Not even worth a penny."

She giggled and squeezed my arm tighter. "Oh, Aaron. You're so silly."

"Come on," I said. "We'd better pick up the pace if we want to make it to the waterfall."

As I said it, the image of Claudia trying to dunk me popped back into my head. I squashed it as quickly as I could, reminding myself that Claudia had chosen soccer over our relationship. She had made it perfectly clear what her priorities were, and I wasn't one of them. So it was pointless to keep thinking about what we used to have.

Stop mooning over your glorious past with Claudia, I told myself as Hilary and I plodded on down the trail, *and start making some memories with Hilary instead.*

"I've got an idea," I told Hilary. "The waterfall's probably only about a mile away now. Why don't we race the rest of the way? Last one there's a rotten egg."

She laughed uncertainly. "You're kidding, right? I mean, we both know there's no way I'd ever beat you."

"Right." I sighed, disappointed by her response. What had I been expecting anyway? "Sure. I was just joking."

I noticed she was giving me a puzzled look. I

forced a smile. "By the way, Hil, you look amazing today. Um, I like your blouse."

Her eyes lit up with pleasure, and she touched the collar of her short-sleeved button-down. "Really? That's sweet of you, Aaron." She reached over and took my hand. "Speaking of clothes, I've been meaning to ask you—do you know what you're wearing to the dance yet?"

"Um, I don't know." The dance was six whole days away. I hadn't even thought about a clothing plan. "Why?"

She rubbed her thumb on my palm. "I want to make sure my dress matches." Smiling up at me, she sighed happily. "I can't wait for next weekend, can you? First the dance on Friday night, then the big game against Westville the next day . . ."

"I thought the football team was playing at Twin Valley next Saturday."

"Oops!" Her cheeks turned pink, and she slapped one hand to her mouth. "I was going to make it a surprise. But I guess you caught me."

"What do you mean?"

She lowered her hand and smiled slyly. "Don't tell anyone," she said. "But I'm going to skip the Twin Valley game so I can go to your soccer game instead." She squeezed my hand. "I know Westville's your biggest rival, and I want to be there to cheer you on."

"Really?" Suddenly all of my petty annoyances disappeared. I tried to imagine what Bruce would say when I told him one of his cheerleaders would rather watch me ride the bench than see him play. "That's great, Hil," I told her sincerely, pulling her toward me. "Thank you."

As I bent to kiss her I couldn't help feeling a little silly about my doubts.

She may not have a lot of her own ideas about things, I thought as she kissed me back eagerly. *But at least she puts me first. At least she's not a pretentious, self-centered know-it-all like Mr. Rebel Without a Clue, Sam Wrightfield.*

Thirteen

Claudia

"THERE'S A SPOT," I said anxiously, pointing straight ahead. "Right there. See it?"

Sam turned to smile at me before steering his car toward the empty parking space in the school lot. "My, my," he said. "You certainly are eager to get there."

No kidding, I thought, clutching the armrest on the door beside me so hard I probably left a mark. *If it were up to me, we would have been at the dance an hour ago, when it started, instead of waiting around to make some kind of dramatic entrance.*

I hadn't thought it was such a terrible idea to arrive a little late, since the DJ the school always hired was known for goofing around and playing weird old songs at the beginning of every dance.

But then, when he'd finally picked me up, Sam had claimed to be so overwhelmed by my beauty that he'd insisted on dancing with me right then and there, in my driveway. It had been cute at first, but Sam didn't let it go. He'd kept us there, humming slow songs and holding me tight, for way too long.

Most girls would probably think that was incredibly romantic, I reminded myself. I glanced at Sam's handsome profile out of the corner of my eye as he finished parking and reached to turn off the car. *Most girls would probably have the sense to appreciate a guy like Sam.*

I just wasn't sure I was one of them. Ever since that double date with Jenna one week earlier, I'd found more and more stupid little things that annoyed me about Sam, from his impromptu public monologues about his pet causes to the way he ran his hands through his hair every five minutes to make sure it was all in place. So far he didn't seem to notice how much he was bugging me, which was pretty irritating too, since I wasn't very good at hiding my feelings.

And now there I was, all dressed up for a romantic evening, feeling agitated because we were a few minutes late. Since when had I become so uptight? I had no idea, but I didn't like it.

Sam climbed out of the car and hurried around to open my door with a flourish. As I got out he put a hand to his heart. "Claudia," he whispered, "you've never looked lovelier."

Jenna and I had gone shopping a few days earlier, and she'd helped me pick out a short, silky, elegant burgundy dress with slender spaghetti straps and a flared skirt. My hair was piled on top of my head, emphasizing my long, slender neck. A few loose tendrils framed my face.

"Thanks," I said lightly, taking the hand he offered. "You don't look too shabby yourself."

That was the truth. Sam looked good in anything he wore, but he was even more striking than usual in his dark sports jacket and crisp white shirt. As we walked into the dance I noticed heads turning to check us out.

I also noticed Aaron.

He was on the dance floor, looking as cute as I'd ever seen him. Whereas Sam looked cool and controlled in his clothes, Aaron seemed free and full of life. I watched as he flung his arms over his head and shook them, grinning as he did what I could only guess was his version of the jitterbug.

Then my gaze turned to his dance partner, and suddenly my pretty burgundy dress didn't feel so special anymore. Hilary wore a sheath of ivory satin that left almost nothing to the imagination. Her reddish blond hair cascaded over her bare shoulders, and her makeup was flawless. I felt a sudden, deep pang of envy as she laughingly grabbed Aaron's arms and pulled them around her waist, turning his solo jitterbug into a dance for two.

I couldn't stand to watch any longer. Turning

to Sam, I grabbed his arm. "Come on," I commanded. "Let's dance."

He looked startled but allowed me to drag him onto the dance floor. I put my arms on his shoulders and started to sway to the beat, moving us step by step toward Aaron and Hilary.

"Oh, Sam," I said loudly. "You're such an awesome dancer!"

"Thanks," he said, still looking a bit puzzled. "Um, it's easy to be a good dancer with such a beautiful partner."

I took another big step backward, wanting to make sure we were close enough for Aaron to hear how crazy Sam and I were about each other. Glancing over my shoulder, I saw that Aaron and Hilary were only a couple of yards away. Neither of them was looking my way, but I was sure they knew we were there. I gazed up at Sam and tightened my arms around his neck, waiting for the compliment that I knew would follow my movement.

"Holding you like this is so special," Sam murmured, right on cue.

I smiled. "Oh, Sam," I exclaimed. "You are *so* romantic. What did I do before I met you?"

"I don't know," he said. He looked a little confused by my sudden, rather loud burst of praise.

I glanced at Aaron again, and this time I caught him sneaking a peek at me. He looked away quickly, but I smiled in triumph. Returning my gaze to Sam, I pressed my body to his, did a sultry wiggle, and tossed my head.

"So, Sam," I continued, "do you know that you are the *most* incredible guy I've ever known?"

"Why don't we move *away* from your ex-boyfriend and his date?" Sam whispered through clenched teeth. My eyes widened, and I felt my cheeks flame up.

"Wh-What do you—" I started to stammer.

"Claudia," a new voice hissed from very close by. Startled, I broke off in midsentence and turned to see Jenna standing there.

"Hey," I greeted her. "You look really gr—"

"Bathroom," she said briskly, grabbing me by the arm. "Now." Tossing Sam a fake smile, she added, "We'll be right back."

She dragged me to the rest room, ignoring a pack of giggling girls swapping lipsticks in front of the mirror. I followed her to the far end of the long, narrow room, feeling a little annoyed at her interruption. "What's up?" I demanded.

"I was just going to ask you the same thing," she said, hiking up her purple velour mini and perching on the old iron radiator. "What was with that performance out there?"

"What are you talking about?"

"You know what I'm talking about." Batting her eyelashes melodramatically, she broke into a shrill squeal. "Ooh, Sam! You're just the manliest man in the entire universe. Hee hee hee hee hee!"

"Give me a break," I told Jenna irritably. "I'm

just trying to have a good time with my new boyfriend. What's wrong with that?"

"What's wrong is that any fool could see you weren't really talking to Sam out there." Jenna folded her arms across her chest and shot me a challenging look. "You were talking to Aaron. Why don't you admit it?"

I faltered for a second, then scowled. "Get real. In case it slipped your mind, Aaron and I broke up. He couldn't handle an equal relationship, which is why he ended up with a mannequin like Hilary Walters."

Jenna sighed and shook her head. "Whatever," she said, sounding exasperated. "I don't know why you can't admit the truth, Claud. What's up with you?" She looked at me for a second, and I didn't respond. I kept my eyes focused on the tiled floor, avoiding her gaze. "Okay," she finally said. "I understand you don't want to talk about it. But you know I'm here for you, right?"

I bit my lip, then nodded quickly, still staring straight down. She sighed, then turned and walked away.

I hesitated before following her out. Jenna knew me way too well. What was I doing? Was I really so insecure and immature that I was willing to make a spectacle of myself just to prove I was over Aaron? That was stupid, not to mention unfair to Sam. After a deep breath and a quick check in the mirror, I headed back to the dance, vowing to keep better control over myself—

physically and emotionally—from then on.

That vow lasted all of half a minute, which was how long it took me to leave the bathroom and recognize the first notes of a familiar slow, romantic song—"Baby, You're Mine." It had been our song, mine and Aaron's. I glanced toward the dance floor and saw that Aaron and Hilary were practically plastered together, slow-dancing as if they were Siamese twins joined at every major organ in their bodies.

All calm, rational thoughts flew out of my head. I had one goal—to make the song end that very second. I spotted Sam standing near where I'd left him, and I raced over. "Listen," I told him breathlessly. "Can you believe what song they're playing?"

Sam shrugged. "Sure, I—"

"We have to stop it," I exclaimed. "We should, uh, we should protest! These lyrics are totally offensive and demeaning to women. It, um, infantilizes them and treats them as male property." The words rushed out of my mouth.

Sam was starting to look interested. "You know, I'd never really thought about it like that," he mused. "I guess you have a point. But then there's that verse where the female singer comes in and—"

"Are we going to stand here and debate, or are we going to make our voices heard?" I cried, catching a glimpse of Aaron and Hilary out of the corner of my eye.

"Okay," Sam said agreeably. "We could go talk to the DJ."

I turned and raced toward the wooden platform at the far end of the room, where the DJ, a heavy-set, bearded man in his forties, had set up his table. Sam followed quickly, passing me just before we reached the DJ.

The music was pretty loud, so I couldn't hear exactly what Sam said to the man. All I could do was watch as the DJ's expression changed from confusion to interest to amusement. Finally Sam stepped back, and the DJ stopped the music and tapped his microphone for attention.

"What did he say?" I asked Sam as he returned to my side. All around us, students were grumbling and pulling apart from their dance partners, shooting annoyed or curious looks at the DJ's table as they wondered what had happened to the music.

Sam shrugged. "He said he'd mention our complaint to the group."

I gulped. I had hoped to put a stop to that particular song and, along with it, the painful sight of watching my replacement dance with my ex-boyfriend to what had been our song. A public forum hadn't been quite what I'd had in mind.

"You didn't give them our names, did y—"

"Ladies and gentlemen!" the DJ's voice boomed out over the room. "I've just received a complaint about the last song from a couple of your schoolmates, a Mr. Sam Wrightfield and Ms. Claudine Willoughby."

"That's Claudia!" Sam called out loudly, putting an arm around me protectively. "Not Claudine—*Claudia.*" I cringed.

The DJ tossed him a sloppy salute in reply. "In any case, these two concerned citizens seem to feel that there's something wrong with 'Baby, You're Mine.'" He paused just long enough to let that sink in. When people started to murmur, he went on. "But we're in America, which means this is a democracy. Does anyone else have a problem with the song?"

There was a chorus of nos from all around us. As I waited to see what would happen next, I idly wondered just exactly how red a person's face had to get before her entire head burst into flames.

The DJ looked smug as he glanced at us. "That's what I thought. Now, since we were so rudely interrupted, I believe I'll put 'Baby, You're Mine' back on now—from the beginning. Enjoy, folks."

A few people cheered. Most just shrugged, laughed, or rolled their eyes and prepared to go back to what they'd been doing. The DJ punched a button, and the opening notes of the ballad poured out over the room again.

Sam quickly leaped toward the DJ's table again. "Just a minute!" he shouted, trying to make himself heard over the music.

The DJ waved a hand at him dismissively, then turned his attention back to his CD pile. But Sam didn't give up that easily. He jumped onto the platform and grabbed the microphone. "My fellow students!" he cried through the sharp whine of feedback. "Don't we have the right to express our opinions about the music here?"

"Give me that!" The DJ swiped at the microphone, his annoyance amplified for all to hear. The music was still playing, but most people had stopped dancing again.

Sam evaded the heavyset man easily, moving with the microphone to the front of the little stage. "That's why I'm asking you to join me in making our voices heard," he announced in his best rabble-rousing tone, walking slowly back and forth across the platform. "We have to show people that we believe men and women should be a team. And what's the best way to do that?" He grinned. "How about a kiss-in?" He shot me a proud glance, gesturing for me to come forward. "Yeah, Claudia and I are going to stand here and *kiss* to demonstrate our solidarity. Anyone else care to join us?"

Oh, my God. What was he doing?

A few people cheered, and there was a lot of laughter. This was, like, a *joke* to everyone—even to Sam! I swallowed hard.

"Yo, man! We'll join your protest!"

"We will too!"

"Yeah! Let's make out for women's rights!"

Sam was still waving for me to join him on the platform. But I couldn't move. I wasn't sure I wanted to kiss Sam in front of the whole school. I suddenly wasn't sure I wanted to kiss Sam at all.

I glanced helplessly toward the spot where I'd last seen Aaron, wondering exactly how I'd gotten myself into this mess. Just as I looked over, I saw Hilary roll her eyes and turn to whisper something in Aaron's ear, putting her hand possessively on his arm.

That was all the encouragement I needed.

I leaped onto the stage and threw my arms around Sam.

Fourteen

Aaron

I COULDN'T BELIEVE Claudia was making such a fool of herself. *That jerk must really be affecting her mind,* I thought. *He must be slipping idiot pills into her cappuccino or something.*

Beside me, Hilary was staring as the two of them started lip-wrestling up there on the DJ's platform. "Can you believe them?" she exclaimed. "Don't they even care that they're ruining the dance for everyone?" She turned to me with a pout. "I mean, I love that song."

"Yeah. This is crazy." I could barely squeeze out the words. It was taking a lot of energy to hide how much it was killing me to see Claudia kissing another guy as our song blared out of the loudspeakers. Every note, every lyric reminded me of what I had lost. I couldn't remember how many times

Claudia and I had danced to it together—once we'd even stopped in the middle of the food court at the mall to sway along with the Muzak version, not caring when dozens of shoppers stopped to stare.

Hilary turned to look at me worriedly. "Don't you think it's a good song, Aaron?" she asked tentatively. "I mean, it's easy to dance to. Right?"

"The song's fine," I said a little harshly. I felt my teeth start to grind together. Why was everything Hilary said that night getting on my nerves so much? Actually, she'd been annoying me all week. It wasn't that she was really doing anything wrong, or even anything different. It was just that her willingness to do whatever I said was feeling—wrong.

At that moment we were all drowned out by the principal's voice booming over the loudspeakers, calling for our attention. Glancing at the DJ stand, I saw that Mr. Carter had grabbed the microphone and was waving his hand at the DJ, who obediently turned off the music.

"Enough of this nonsense," the principal said sternly, glaring first at Claudia and the dork and then at some of the other couples who had joined in the protest. All of them stopped kissing and turned to listen to him. "Your so-called protest is over—unless you want this dance to be over. And I think we've had enough of that song too."

"More than enough!" Sam called, his arm slung around Claudia's shoulders.

The principal ignored the comment. He pointed to the DJ. "Let's pick up the tempo now, shall we?"

The DJ shrugged and stuck another CD into his machine. Seconds later, the lively beat of a recent hit poured out of the speakers.

The principal watched for a moment as Claudia and the loser climbed down from the platform and most of the other kids started dancing. Then he disappeared into the crowd again.

"It's about time somebody put a stop to that ridiculous protest." Hilary sounded so self-righteous, it probably would have made me nuts if I'd been paying full attention to her. But Claudia and Sam were making their way past us at the moment, and seeing him walking along with his arm slung casually around her shoulder, looking smug, went straight to my head. Suddenly the only thing that seemed important was proving to everyone, especially Claudia, that their pathetic make-out session hadn't bothered me one bit.

"Well, that was a big waste of time," I announced at the top of my lungs, wanting to be sure they heard me over the pounding beat of the music.

Out of the corner of my eye, I saw Claudia's head turn. I knew I had her attention, so I plowed on, hardly knowing what I was going to say until the words came out.

"That so-called protest cheated me of a slow dance with the most beautiful girl in school," I continued. "I won't stand for it. Hilary, would you do me the honor?"

She looked confused at first, but when I took her in my arms and started swaying, totally ignoring the pounding beat of the music, she caught on. "Oh, Aaron," she sighed happily.

I pressed her more tightly to me, running my hands slowly over her bare shoulders and back. As I saw Claudia spin on her heel and drag Sam away, I knew I'd made my point, and then some.

So why did it feel so lousy?

Fifteen

Claudia

I WOKE UP the next morning with a sick feeling in my stomach. As I rolled onto my back and stared up at the ceiling, I remembered why. The dance hadn't been some wacky, surrealistic dream. That had really been me up there, making out with Sam in front of the whole school.

I groaned and sat up, wishing my head weren't suddenly crammed with unpleasant images: Sam whirling me around the dance floor, suggesting a kiss-in for peace and a make-out march on Washington, and Aaron and Hilary glued to each other as if an inch of space between them would have been a huge tragedy.

Pushing away the terrible memories, I dragged myself out of bed and down the hall to the bathroom to get ready for the big soccer game.

Soccer—the one thing that made sense. Why couldn't everything else be so simple and natural? When I was on the field, I always knew exactly what my next move should be. But just then I had no idea *what* to do about the rest of my life.

I grabbed my toothbrush and started brushing my teeth vigorously, staring at my reflection in the mirror and wondering when things had gotten so out of control. Sam had seemed like every girl's dream come true, with all of his passion and romance. And maybe he was—but maybe I just wasn't every girl. It was clear now that Sam and I weren't right for each other.

Then there was Aaron.

Despite everything he had done to me, I couldn't stop thinking about the way things used to be between us. I couldn't stop missing him, and I certainly couldn't stop hating the fact that he was with Hilary.

Ugh, it was just so endlessly confusing. *Soccer,* I reminded myself as I turned on the water in the shower. *Just focus on the game today, and then figure out the rest later.* I hoped that would be easier than it seemed.

I jogged onto the field for the start of the game, shading my eyes and peering up into the stands, searching for familiar faces. I spotted my parents first—they'd driven me over for warm-up and then hung around, talking to some of the other parents sitting in the first few rows of bleachers. When Dad saw me looking his way, he stood and waved both arms over his head, grinning. I grinned back, and he gave me a thumbs-up.

Sam would have arrived a little later, so I moved my gaze higher. The stands were much more crowded than they'd been for our scrimmages. The first official game of the season was always a big deal, but that day we were playing Westville, our biggest rival, so the stands were really crammed.

I saw Jenna sitting with Greg and some of our other friends, but Sam wasn't with them. Finally I spotted him. He was sitting by himself at the end of the fourth row of bleachers, a black muffler wrapped around his neck as if he were cold, even though the weather was mild. He didn't look particularly comfortable, and I cringed at the reminder of how much he didn't fit in here, in my world. When he saw me looking his way, he smiled and waved.

I was raising my arm to return his wave when someone slammed into me from behind. "Oof!" I exclaimed as the breath whooshed out of my body.

"Sorry," Jason Kent said as I turned to glare at him. He didn't look sorry at all. "Didn't see you there, Willoughby."

"Right," I muttered, resisting the urge to snap out an insult. A lot of the guys on the team still hadn't adjusted to my presence, but I was learning to live with it. I wasn't going to let any of them blow my focus—not when we were playing Westville.

I turned to size up their team as they came onto

the field. They looked pretty tough, but I was feeling confident. We could beat them.

Coach Baker called us together for a last-minute pep talk. My heart started to pound as the entire team gathered in a big circle at the edge of the field.

I found myself standing directly across the huddle from Aaron. He met my eye for a second before quickly moving his gaze to its usual position these days, which seemed to be somewhere about six inches above my right shoulder. I felt a twinge of some kind of emotion but shoved it down immediately. I had other things to think about at the moment.

Focus, I told myself. I tuned in to what Coach Baker was saying, forgetting everything else.

After giving us the usual encouraging words, the coach clapped his hands. "Okay, people," he said briskly. "I don't have to tell you that this is an important game. So let's do it. Let's win this thing!"

As we all let out a cheer, I could feel the adrenaline coursing through my veins, the way it always did in those last few minutes before the start of a game. I headed onto the field with the other starters, making my way into position.

At last the game started. I was itching to get my feet on the ball, but I didn't get a chance for the first few minutes of play. One of the Westville strikers was quick enough to whisk it right past Joel Wyman at the other side of the field, passing to a teammate, who drove down the center of the field. Our defenders were ready, and he didn't get far.

Rich Tarvell threatened the Westville player enough to make him panic, and when he tried to pass, his kick was wild, sending the ball out of bounds.

A Westville player collected the ball after the throw-in and dodged past one of our midfielders. After that their team did some impressive passing, keeping the ball out of our reach but failing to move it very far down the field toward our goal.

Just when I was starting to wonder if they were even going to try to score, one of the Westville players took the ball and feinted past two of our guys. Before any of us quite knew what was happening, he'd found a clear shot and taken it. Jason leaped for the ball, but it bounced off his hands and flew into the side of the net. Home team 0, visitors 1.

It took a few minutes, but we eventually got our revenge for that goal with one of our own. This time I got to play a part, receiving a long pass from a midfielder, dribbling neatly past the player who was marking me, and then passing the ball to Charlie Donnelly, who scored.

After that, there were no goals for a long time, though there was plenty of action. Neither side gave an inch. The ball flew back and forth, up and down the field. We took our best shots, but the goalies knew what they were doing, and they thwarted all attempts to break the early 1–1 tie.

The first half of the game flew by. I'd forgotten I was the only girl on the team. I'd forgotten everything else except my burning desire to put that black-and-white ball into my opponent's goal.

There was less than a minute left before the half-time break when I saw my chance. Joel had the ball and had managed to move it almost into striking distance. Charlie and I were both right there with him. But Charlie was being closely guarded, while I was free and clear.

I could see that Joel was getting into some trouble. Two Westville defenders were all over him, and he had nowhere to go. He either had to take the ball out of bounds, try for an almost impossible shot at the goal, or pass to Charlie or me.

"Wyman!" I screamed as loudly as I could. I waved my hands over my head and bounced on the balls of my feet. "I'm open! I'm open!"

Joel glanced my way, then looked over at Charlie, who was still being shadowed. I knew what Joel was thinking. He had been one of the most resistant to my presence on the team from the beginning, but now he was finally being put on the spot. He didn't want to pass to me. Not to a girl. But if he didn't . . .

He was looking for another way out. If Charlie had been free, there would have been no problem. But Charlie was well covered. Joel dribbled more or less in place for a long moment, obviously considering his options.

I couldn't believe he was being so stubborn, but I didn't have time to get angry about it then. I just had to get through to him. "Wyman!" I shrieked again. "Over here!"

Glancing to the side, I saw a red-haired Westville player racing up the field in my direction. Apparently he'd just noticed that no one was guarding me. It was now or never.

"Wyman!"

This time Joel reacted. Feinting out of reach of a Westville player who was moving in for a steal, he kicked the ball toward me, fast and straight. I leaped forward to meet the ball, deflecting it expertly off my knee and, in the same move, turning toward the goal.

The redhead was almost upon me. I had to move fast, and I did, my body acting automatically. I dribbled for half a second, making sure I was ready, judging the goalie's position. Then I took my shot, putting my weight into the kick and curving the ball toward the goal.

The goalie charged forward, but he misjudged the arc of the ball. It flew right over his head, whooshing into the back of the net—a clean, perfect shot.

"All right!" Charlie Donnelly's voice rose above the cries of the crowd and the buzz of the timer ending the first half. He raced over and flung his arms around me, lifting me off the ground in an excited bear hug.

Before I knew it, the rest of the team was upon us. I felt half a dozen hands slapping me on the back. Voices were calling my name. A moment later

Jason grabbed me by the waist and hoisted me into the air. Other arms reached to help support me, and the amazing truth dawned on me.

They had finally accepted me. I was part of the team at last!

I hadn't realized how much that meant to me until it was finally happening. Tears sprang to my eyes, but I was smiling too hard to let them fall. As I clutched Jason's square head to keep from toppling off the shoulders supporting me, I heard myself whooping with the joy of victory. I'd never felt so fantastic in my entire life.

Until I saw Aaron.

I happened to glance toward the sidelines, and there he was. He hadn't come over to join the celebration with the rest of the guys. Instead, he sat alone on the bench, staring toward me with a strange, wistful smile on his face.

A stab of guilt pierced my heart.

This could have been his celebration, if it weren't for me.

I felt as if I were seeing clearly for the first time in weeks. The thrill of playing in our first actual game of the season really brought home everything that Aaron was missing out on. Maybe soccer wasn't as important to him as it was to me, but this used to be his world. The guys holding me up were Aaron's friends—and when I'd decided to try out for the team, I'd invaded that part of his life without listening to his fears about how things would change for him.

How could I have done that to someone I was supposed to love?

When Aaron saw me looking his way, his face cleared and he gave me a thumbs-up. After all that had happened, he was actually *happy* for me. Because of me he was there on the bench instead of out on the field scoring his own goals, but he could still support my victory. *Because he knows what this moment means to me,* I realized, my heart rate speeding up. *He knows better than anyone.*

All the love I felt for Aaron and which I'd buried since we broke up came rushing to the surface. I had never even been *close* to getting over him—how could I have thought that was possible, when he was so perfect for me?

Suddenly my triumph didn't feel as wonderful. Suddenly all I wanted was to tell Aaron how sorry I was for never listening to his feelings.

When the guys finally lowered me to the ground, I started to head in Aaron's direction. But before I got far, my dad raced down off the bleachers and grabbed me in a big hug. "Brilliant!" he exclaimed. He looked around at the nearby spectators hanging out at the sidelines. "Check it out, everyone. This is my brilliant daughter!"

Brilliant? I wouldn't have used that word to describe my actions over the past few weeks.

My dad finally finished fussing over me and climbed back up to sit with my mom in the stands, and I anxiously looked around for Aaron. I couldn't find him, but I did spot Sam striding in my direction. I gulped and forced a smile. In all the excitement and emotion of the last few minutes, I'd forgotten all about Sam.

What could I say to him? How could I have expected to connect with Sam the way I had with Aaron? How could I have imagined I could care about him even half as much?

"I didn't want to interrupt you and your dad," Sam explained when he reached me, bending to give me a quick peck on the cheek. "So I waited to congratulate you."

"Thanks. He's pretty excited, as you could probably tell."

"Looks like he's not the only one." Sam glanced around at my teammates, most of whom were still whooping and hollering and slapping each other high fives nearby. His nose wrinkled slightly. "The way they're carrying on, you'd think this game really mattered."

For a second I wasn't certain that I'd heard him right. "What did you say?"

Sam realized his mistake immediately. "That's not what I meant," he said quickly, giving my arm a squeeze. "It does matter—it matters a lot. You've really proved that a woman can compete equally with—"

"That's not why it matters to me." I cut him off furiously, shaking my arm free of his grasp. All my pent-up annoyance with him was boiling over at last, and this time I could tell I wasn't going to be able to stop it. I didn't *want* to stop it. "It matters to me because it's what I do. It's what I love."

"Sure." Sam looked uncertain. "Of course. I understand."

"I don't think you do." I was shaking, though my voice sounded remarkably steady. "I don't think you really understand me at all. And I *know* I don't understand you."

Sam looked shocked. "What are you saying?"

"I'm saying I don't think we should see each other anymore."

"Claudia," Sam said in his calmest, most rational voice, "please be reasonable. I don't think you know what you're saying."

I just folded my arms across my chest and stared at him, using what Aaron had always called my spontaneous-combustion look.

Sam met my gaze for a few seconds, then looked away. Running a hand through his dark blond hair, he sighed and shook his head.

"Fine," he said shortly. "If that's the way you want it."

He spun on his heel and stalked off without a backward look. I watched him go, feeling a little sad, a little angry—but mostly just relieved. Now that it was over, I couldn't really believe my three-week relationship with Sam had actually happened. It had been a huge mistake to think we could ever be right for each other.

And a huge mistake to think I was over Aaron, I thought. Of course Sam couldn't make me happy. I didn't want his romantic gestures—I wanted Aaron.

I knew now without a doubt that Aaron was the one for me, but he'd already moved on. Still, I had to at least let him know how sorry I was for what I had done.

I turned to search the crowds gathered along the edge of the field.

Before I could locate Aaron, Jenna hurried toward me. "Awesome action, girl!" she exclaimed, smacking me soundly on the shoulder. Then she paused, peering into my face. "What's the matter?"

"Sam and I are through."

Jenna's eyes widened. "Wow." She scratched her cheek. "Um, I don't know what to say."

I grimaced at her. "Go ahead," I said wearily. "You can be happy about it. It's okay."

"Cool." Jenna broke out into a grin. "Then let me be the first to congratulate you on your second brilliant play of the afternoon!" She put an arm around my shoulders and hugged me comfortingly. "Sorry. Couldn't resist. But you know I'm here for you."

"I know." I smiled weakly at her. "I just wish you could tell me what to do about Aaron."

"Aaron?" Jenna's ears pricked up at that. "What do you mean?"

"Are you going to make me say it?" I sighed. "All right. I think I really messed up with him."

"You mean it?" Jenna looked thrilled. "Awesome! So why are you standing around talking to me? Go find him."

"I don't know." I hesitated, my eyes wandering

as I started searching for him again. There was a big knot of people over near our bench, and I couldn't see him, though I was sure he was over there somewhere. "What's the point? It's too late. He's with Hilary now."

Jenna bit her lip. "True." She tugged at a curl that had escaped from her ponytail. "So are you really just going to sit back and let her have him? That doesn't sound like you."

"It doesn't, does it?" I felt a flicker of my usual determination flare up. Jenna was right. I wasn't the type to just sit back and give up, not when there was even the slightest chance of getting what I'd finally figured out I really wanted. Maybe Aaron was in love with Hilary now. But maybe he wasn't. And if he wasn't . . . "I'll catch you later, okay?"

Leaving Jenna, I started to push my way through the crowds. There were only a few minutes of halftime remaining. I had to find Aaron and talk to him. Now that everything was finally clear to me, I couldn't waste another second before letting Aaron know how I felt.

Sixteen

Aaron

AFTER STARING IN awe at Claudia's incredible play, I was so blown away I couldn't move. I just sat there on the bench, totally overcome, and watched as the other guys carried Claudia around the field. Her action had been flawless, her shot clean—it was one of the greatest goals I'd ever seen.

Even though observing the game from the bench was really hard, I couldn't help but feel caught up in Claudia's victory. When she had looked at me, I'd given her a thumbs-up without even thinking twice. My instinctive response was to show her how proud I was.

Wait—was that really true? How could I be proud of the girl who had chosen her position on the soccer team over our relationship? Actually, the girl who had chosen *my* position on the soccer team over our relationship.

Somehow that thought didn't send my temper into overdrive the way it usually did.

Maybe because you were the idiot who forced her to choose.

The thought popped into my head and made such perfect sense that I couldn't believe it had taken me this long to see it. Claudia was an unbelievable soccer player. Watching the way she moved out there, I found it impossible to deny that she and soccer were meant for each other. How could I have asked her to give up something she was so good at, that made her so happy? Something that she even planned to do with her *life?*

I couldn't watch the action on the field anymore. Rubbing my face with both hands, I squeezed my eyes shut and shook my head sadly.

I'd blown it. I'd really blown it this time.

I had to talk to her. I had to congratulate her on her awesome first half, and then I had to apologize for acting like such a jerk. I couldn't lie to myself for a second longer—I still loved her. Even if she was blissfully happy with Wrightfield now and I'd lost my chance for good, I had to at least make up for what I'd done.

I hopped off the bench and started pushing my way past the excited players and spectators who were standing around the sidelines talking about the game. I heard Claudia's name flying around everywhere, which only made me more eager to find her and make things right between us if I could.

But before I found Claudia, Hilary found me.

"Aaron!" she exclaimed, clutching my arm. "There you are. It's such a madhouse around here that I thought I'd never find you."

"Yeah," I said, demonstrating my usual brilliant repartee. What could I say to her? I knew I couldn't be with her anymore, but now wasn't the time to have this conversation.

Hilary was glancing around at the crowds surrounding us, shaking her head in disbelief. "Can you believe the big deal everyone is making over Claudia?"

"I know," I replied, looking around nervously. "It's pretty amazing. She's probably got this year's MVP award sewn up after that play."

Hilary looked at me suspiciously, probably confused that I didn't share her outrage. "Very funny," she said. "I mean, the game is only half over, and the way people are acting, you'd think Claudia had just single-handedly won the state championship or something." She wrinkled her nose. "They all seem to have forgotten one very important fact: She's a girl. And a girl shouldn't be allowed to play on a guys' team. No matter what."

Something inside me snapped. Maybe it was what she'd said. Maybe it was the way she'd said it—with that smug look on her face, as if she personally set all the rules for the world's behavior. Or maybe it was just the fact that she'd interrupted me when I was trying to find the girl I really loved.

"Get real, Hilary," I barked. "If you were any

kind of strong woman yourself, you'd respect Claudia for going after what she wants, for having the courage to stand up for herself. Maybe you should take a few lessons on that from her. Believe me, you could use them."

From the shocked and wounded expression on her face, you'd have thought I'd run her down with a Mack truck and then backed over her a few times. Her blue eyes widened and immediately filled with tears. Within seconds those tears were rolling down her face in huge, round droplets, and her lower lip was quivering.

"Oh!" she exclaimed. "Oh!"

I immediately felt guilty. None of this was Hilary's fault, and it wasn't fair to take it out on her. She was basically a nice person who just didn't happen to be right for me.

"I'm sorry," I said, putting my arm around her. She started to push me away, then apparently thought better of it. Collapsing against my chest, she broke into loud sobs.

"There, there." I felt foolish as I helplessly patted her back with both hands.

Why do people say that anyway? I wondered as I waited for her to regain control of herself. *What exactly does 'there, there' mean? Probably 'There, there, go over there so I don't have to deal with your hysterics.' At least that's what I mean by it now.*

I wished I could just shove her aside and continue my search for Claudia. The clock was ticking, and halftime would be over all too soon. I didn't think I could survive sitting through the rest of the game without talking to her. But it was my fault that Hilary was so upset, so I held back my impatience the best I could.

Finally she looked up at me, her face streaked with tears. "Aaron . . ."

I didn't let her go on. I didn't want her to get the wrong idea about why I had my arms around her. "Hilary," I said as gently as I could, "I'm so sorry about what I just said. I didn't mean to be so harsh. It's just that I wasn't sure how to tell you that . . . I don't think things are going to work out between us."

"What do you mean?" Her voice trembled slightly.

I gulped, hating every second of this. "You're a really cool person, Hilary. It's been great getting to know you. But I don't think we should see each other anymore."

She didn't answer. She just looked at me and nodded, and the tears started rolling again.

What could I do? I wasn't totally heartless. And I couldn't help feeling a little bit sad when I remembered all the nice things she had said to me, all the kind things she had done. So I put my arms around her one last time, for one last hug. She clutched me as if she never wanted to let me go. But this time I knew we both understood that it was over.

Seventeen

Claudia

W*HERE IS HE?* I fought my way through the crowd, finally breaking out of it in time to see a scene that stopped my heart cold. Aaron was half a dozen yards away, in a little clearing just beyond the halftime crowd on the sidelines.

But he wasn't alone. Hilary was with him, and apparently they'd totally forgotten that they were in public, with tons of people around. Her back was to me, and Aaron had his arms wrapped around her, slowly rubbing her neck. His face was half buried in her shoulder, blocked partially from my view by her strawberry blond hair. But I could see enough to note that his eyes were squeezed shut and his face looked totally serious.

I felt a sinking sensation in the pit of my stomach, a thousand times worse than the one I got when I flubbed a shot in a game. It was too late. I had realized too late that Aaron was the only guy for me.

As I turned away and moved off blindly through the crowd, I realized that even if Aaron was with Hilary now, even if we couldn't be together, I still loved him. I still wanted him to be happy—and there was a way I could make that happen.

I glanced out at the field. Most of my teammates were starting to drift away from the crowd at the sidelines. Taking a deep breath, I jogged toward them, wanting to make sure I had an audience for what I was about to do. I felt a little queasy, but I quickly suppressed the feeling. There was no other way.

I waited until I was only a few yards away from the home bench. Gathering up all of my paltry acting skills, I suddenly let out an ear-piercing shriek and pitched forward, then immediately rolled over and clutched my ankle.

"Ow!" I yelled. "Ouch! My ankle!" I squeezed my face up, using the pain of knowing I'd lost Aaron to substitute for the physical pain I was trying to fake.

Coach Baker and the other players were already racing toward me. The coach dropped to his knees beside me and reached tentatively toward my ankle. I wasn't sure I could really make the sacrifice of quitting the sport I loved entirely—but I figured I could at least give this game to Aaron.

"What's the matter? Claudia, what happened?"

At the familiar voice, my eyes flew open. Aaron

had arrived on the scene and was kneeling beside the coach, gazing at me with open concern in his deep brown eyes.

"Aaron," I breathed before I could stop myself. Suddenly remembering where I was and what I was doing, I let out a fake sob. "I—I tripped and twisted my ankle. I don't think I can play the second half."

Aaron leaned a little closer. He wasn't looking at my ankle—he was still gazing directly into my face. Suddenly he sat up and glanced around at the coach and the other onlookers. "It's okay," he said briskly. "I think she'll be fine. Just give us a second, will you?"

"I won't be fine," I insisted, grimacing as dramatically as I could as I continued to grasp my ankle. "My leg . . ."

"Stop it." Aaron was looking at me again. He lifted one hand and brushed a strand of hair off my face. "You should know better than to try to fool me with that Pinocchio face of yours. I know you better than anyone, remember?"

I just stared at him for a moment, forgetting even to grimace or groan. His face and voice were so tender that I wasn't sure how to respond.

Aaron turned away again long enough to shoo the others back. Then he grabbed me by both arms and dragged me to my feet. I was too startled to carry on my charade any longer, and as soon as Coach Baker saw me standing squarely on both legs, his face cleared.

"I think maybe these two have something to say to each other," the coach told our teammates gruffly. He glanced at me, then at Aaron. "Just don't take too long. We've got a team huddle in a couple of minutes." He herded the other guys away.

"Aaron," I said softly when we were alone. Standing this close to him made me forget almost everything else. "I wanted to—I wanted you to be able to—"

"I know." He cut me off by touching one finger briefly to my lips. "I know exactly what you were doing, and I totally appreciate the gesture. But why? I've been such a jerk, and I—"

"No," I said quickly. "No, I was the jerk. I didn't think about what my joining the team would do to you. I never meant to take away your position, but I—"

"Claud, you *deserve* the position. You're an incredible soccer player." He shook his head. "Watching you out there makes it all so obvious. It was awful of me to try to keep you off the team. I'm sorry for everything I've put you through. Really."

I stared into Aaron's sweet, open face. "It serves me right that you found Hilary and I ended up alone," I said sadly.

"Wait a minute." Aaron grasped my arms again and looked intently into my eyes. "Alone? But what about Sam? I thought you two were crazy about each other."

"That's over." I sighed, thinking about what a fool I'd been. "Sam wasn't right for me. I should have known that all along, but I was too stubborn to see it."

"Hilary and I are over too," Aaron said. "I just told her."

"You what?" I could hardly believe my ears. "But I thought you two were so happy together."

Aaron shook his head. "How could I be happy with her?" he asked softly. "How could I ever be happy with anyone but you, Claud?"

I didn't know what to say. Emotions were rolling through me one after the other, so fast I could hardly keep track. "Oh, Aaron," I breathed.

"I just wish I'd realized this sooner," he went on earnestly, tightening his grip on my arms slightly. "I shouldn't have made you choose between soccer and me—that wasn't fair. I know now that I'd rather sit on the bench, cheering on my girlfriend the star, than be a mediocre starting player myself." He glanced down at the ground, then met my eyes again. "I was just scared that if you could choose soccer so easily, it meant I was never that important to you."

I was so overwhelmed that I couldn't speak for a moment. "I never realized you doubted how I felt about you," I said at last.

He shrugged. "I'm a dork, I guess," he said quietly. "But—I guess I just needed more reassurance that my feelings mattered to you." He smiled shyly. "Of course, treating you like I did at tryouts wasn't the best way to get it."

I felt the corners of my mouth turning up, and I let out a giggle. Soon we were both laughing, and it was so natural—so *right.*

"Hey," Aaron said when we'd both settled down, "it looks like our team needs us."

We were standing on the playing field, just outside the home goal box. Most of the other people had cleared off the sidelines, returning to the stands. Our team was lined up near the bench, and most of the guys were watching Aaron and me curiously, though they were too far away to overhear us. The coach was motioning for us to come back for the pep talk.

"It looks like it's time to show you how much I love you. And I'm going to start right now."

Pulling Aaron to me, I kissed him with every ounce of love I had, right there for everyone to see. He kissed me back, and I knew that nothing that had happened between us in the past few weeks mattered. All that counted was that we were back together where we both belonged, and that we were going to stay that way.

Do you ever wonder about falling in love? About members of the opposite sex? Do you need a little friendly advice but have no one to turn to? Well, that's where we come in . . . Jenny and Jake. Send us those questions you're dying to ask, and we'll give you the straight scoop on life and love.

DEAR JAKE

Q: *While working at a summer camp, I met this really sweet guy and we became a couple. But a few days before camp ended, he told me he had a girlfriend back at home and couldn't continue our relationship post-camp. When school started, he called to tell me that he and his girlfriend broke up and that he'd like to see me again. I really like him and want to ask him to my junior prom, but after the way he treated me, I'm not sure about him. What should I do?*

RN, Bruce, WI

A: I can understand why you're hesitant to ask him to the prom—after what happened over the summer, who can blame you? But while you have every right to be doubtful of his intentions, holding on to a bad past experience may not be the way to go. Sounds to me as if you two need to have a long and hard conversation—ask him why he deceived you over the summer, why he and his girlfriend broke up, why he suddenly wants to see you again. If you feel he's being honest and you want to give him a second chance, start picking out that prom dress!

DEAR JENNY

Q: *My boyfriend and I have been dating for two months. He's captain of the football team and very popular. The problem is his ex-girlfriend. She flirts with him constantly and he flirts back. When they're not flirting with each other, they're talking on the phone or hanging out together. When I confronted him about it, he told me I have nothing to worry about and that I was being paranoid. My friends say I should dump him. I'm not sure what to do because I really care about him. Do you think I'm being paranoid? Should I break up with him?*

HM, Detroit, MI

A: I don't think you're being paranoid at all. As a matter of fact, I think you've been very patient, considering your boyfriend's behavior. If I were in your place, I would be reacting the same way. After all, not only has he not offered you an explanation as to why he is suddenly spending so much time with his ex, but he is being completely insensitive to your feelings about the whole thing. If you really think the relationship is worth saving, try talking to your boyfriend again. Don't let him dismiss it by telling you that you're being paranoid. If the relationship he has with his ex is just an innocent friendship, then he should be willing to discuss it with you.

Do you have questions about love? Write to:

Jenny Burgess or Jake Korman
c/o 17th Street Productions,
a division of Daniel Weiss Associates, Inc.
33 West 17th Street
New York, NY 10011

SUPER EDITIONS

Listen to My Heart . . . . Katherine Applegate
Kissing Caroline . . . . Cheryl Zach
It's Different for Guys . . . . Stephanie Leighton
My Best Friend's Girlfriend . . . . Wendy Loggia
Love Happens . . . . Elizabeth Chandler
Out of My League . . . . Everett Owens
A Song for Caitlin . . . . J.E. Bright
The "L" Word . . . . Lynn Mason
Summer Love . . . . Wendy Loggia
All That . . . . Lynn Mason

Coming soon:

#41 *How Do I Tell?* . . . . Kieran Scott